D0926346

THE BOY WHO
SWALLOWS FLIES

Michael F. Stewart

THE BOY WHO SWALLOWS FLIES

By Michael F. Stewart

www.michaelfstewart.com

Praise for *Keep in a Cold, Dark Place*

"With its tyrannical parents, moronic siblings, goofy monsters, and dark humor, the book summons the works of middle-grade master Roald Dahl.

A darkly funny rural tale with a scary bent." —*Kirkus Reviews*

Praise for *Counting Wolves*

"Stewart lets the story do the talking in a world populated by fabulous supporting characters and full of surprises. Counting Wolves is an engaging read for teens and adults alike," Wesley King, author of the Silver Birch Award and Edgar Award winner OCDaniel.

Praise for *Assured Destruction*

"A fun, fast-paced thriller guaranteed to distract teens from Facebook ..." —*Kirkus Reviews*

For my larvae

Chapter 1
Where Jarrod Has No Thing

I toss Gavin the race car game piece. Whenever we play Monopoly, he's always the race car. I'm usually the top hat, but today, I have a surprise.

Gavin perches at the edge of his chair, curly hair burnished copper by the sunlight streaming through his living-room window. Gavin and his family go to Ireland every summer, returning the day before school starts with a hint of Irish lilt in their voices. I haven't seen him for months, and a lot has changed. He's not much taller, but he's thinner and seems older. Older than me.

"Not wanting the top hat?" he asks.

We're at his house. I don't really want to be at my house right now. I finally handed my parents my report card from summer school—I didn't do well.

"Just wait," I say in response to Gavin's quizzical look, and search in my knapsack for the glass jar.

"Not Monopoly again." Gavin's older sister walks into the living room, cocks a hip in a way I don't remember her doing at the beginning of summer, and shakes her head. "Why don't you play video games like other kids?"

I find the jar and hold it aloft. Inside scrabbles my cockroach, a Madagascar hissing cockroach.

Gavin and his sister squint at it, and then she squeezes her head between the palms of her hands.

"Get *that* out of here," she shouts.

I wink at Gavin and spin off the lid.

"Roachie's awesome," I say, shaking the large bug into my hand. It's as long as my thumb and chocolate brown.

"What's that for?" Gavin asks, staring at it sidelong.

"I know why you're not like other kids," his sister screams. "Because you're both gross losers! Mom!" And then she darts away.

"Don't worry," I say. "I've trained him to act like a game piece. Watch."

I place my roachie on "Go" and then toss the game die. I roll a five.

I tap the board five times, and Roachie moves five spaces to land on Reading Railroad.

"Isn't that so cool?" I ask.

Gavin lifts an eyebrow, his eyes twinkling. "I'm afraid that isn't very efficient."

"Oh, come on, a trained roachie? I bet there are scientists who'd be interested in this."

"Uh huh." Gavin's hand slaps down on the game board, causing the die to bounce. "Wait—where'd the roach go?"

Gavin's mom and sister step into the room.

"Jarrod," his mom says. "I appreciate your love for insects, but would ask you contain that love to your own home."

I spot Roachie. They really can be quick. He's making his

way across the living-room floor . . . toward Gavin's mom.

"Sorry—" I say.

"There, there, there!" his sister shouts, hiding behind her mother and pointing. "Get it!"

Gavin's mom stomps her foot around, but her eyes are closed and she keeps missing. I rush to stand overtop of my buddy. Both Gavin's mom and sister do a little jog on the spot and then retreat down the hall.

I sigh and scoop Roachie into his jar.

"So misunderstood," I say, screwing the lid back on. "Sorry about all the screaming, little guy."

"You're talking to them now?" Gavin asks.

"Do you talk to your dog?" I reply.

"Sure, but he's a dog."

"Roachie can be trained. It's a pet. It should live almost as long as a dog. What's the difference?" I hold the roachie up so that the jar blazes in the setting sun.

"You really don't see a difference," he says. It's not a question. "Cockroaches are *not* man's best friend."

"Why not?" I ask.

Gavin nods to the hallway down which his mother and sister disappeared.

I shrug. It's not like I need another way to repel girls. The helmet I wear is equally effective. I pick up the top hat game piece and place it on "Go." "So, are we going to play or what?"

"You have any more syncope this week?" Gavin's a bit of a show-off and is always using big words. Syncope: unexplained losses of consciousness. I faint regularly. Hence the helmet.

Solving the mystery of my passing out, aka my "syncopes," or what my mother calls my "moments," is a favorite of his. For a kid as smart as Gavin, a mystery he can't solve is hard to find.

"Nothing since my last email."

"Ah, the face-in-pie incident." He nods.

"One of my sweeter moments," I say.

He laughs at that.

"Punny," he replies and then gets all serious. "I only have one more year to solve the mystery," he adds, not showing any real interest in playing.

"It's the last year we'll be at the same school," I say, "not last year we'll be friends." Once we reach high school, the gifted kids go to a totally different school. I won't see much of him, but that doesn't mean we can't hang out, right?

"This year's going to be savage," he says, ignoring my comment. Even though I know savage means amazing in Ireland, his voice seems flat, and he keeps glancing toward Roachie as if it'll escape. He used to like my bugs.

Gavin and I have been best friends since third grade. Every year since, he's needed me a little less and I've needed him a little more. Especially after I donned my helmet. Who else do I have other than my bugs?

"Why do you hang out with me?" I ask. "I mean, you're the smartest kid in the whole school and I'm the dumbest. It makes no sense."

Gavin gives me the sort of look I expect from a wise old man. He really is smart.

"Not dumb," he says. "You're probably almost as smart as me, only you haven't found your aptitude."

"My aptitude."

"Yeah. Your thing."

What if I don't have an aptitude? I don't voice my fear aloud because this is enough self-pity for one conversation.

"So, what's *your* thing?" I ask.

Gavin doesn't hesitate. "My thing? It's being smart. I like being the smart kid."

"Isn't that shallow?"

"I guess, but it's mine. I own it. I think that's what's important about your thing. That it's yours and you really don't care what even best friends think about it—at least, not too much."

"Sorry."

It's awkward for a second, and I pat Roachie's lid.

"No worries. Eat two bugs as penance," he says.

"No way, but your dog's looking tasty."

We laugh together, but we don't play any Monopoly. I leave with a promise that he'll play with me tomorrow morning at school. It's our thing, I guess. At least, I hope it still is.

Chapter 2
Where Jarrod Has a Moment

I hit the kitchen floor, my helmet knocking hard. One moment I'd been eating crispy rice cereal and the next, *Bang!* Off the chair I fell. I should be staring at the whirling ceiling fan, but I'm not. I am having a moment. What I call a nightmare. Gavin thinks they're out-of-body experiences. It's tough to argue with that because instead of seeing the kitchen, where I lie unconscious, I see our living room.

I look down on my mom as she flutters my summer school report card in my father's face. My dad sits, feet up on a stool, watching football. It's like I'm dead, but I'm not, or at least I know I won't be for long. It only ever lasts a moment.

"Cs and Ds, Arnie." My mom waggles the paper. "You weren't good in school either, were you? No one in *my* family has difficulty maintaining attention."

"I thought summer school was supposed to be easier?" Dad mutes the television and plucks the report from her fingers. "He really failed physical education? Who fails P.E.?"

"He didn't fail. He got an E," Mom says.

"Never heard of an E . . ." Dad scratches his belly.

"I'm more worried about the D in math. He won't even get a job in retail."

"Nothing wrong with retail," Dad says. "I work retail."

"Selling cars is different. He'll at least need a high school diploma for that, and that doesn't seem likely."

Hey, I want to scream. *I have an A! My first A.* But this is like a vivid dream. I can't say anything. Just like I can't stop it. I'm not even here, more like a fly on the wall.

"He does have one A," my father says. "Says here that Mr. Chang wants to move Jarrod to gifted science."

Thanks, Dad.

The bark of my mother's laugh dismisses my A. "Do you realize what they talked about in science this summer? I bet you can guess. Guess. Go ahead and guess."

"Bugs?"

"Bugs." My mother swats at the report as if it's some irritating gnat. "He'll be crushed in gifted. I don't think we should allow it."

Dad's eyes follow the football on the screen. "He'll be okay. Did you know you can't actually fail eighth grade anymore? They won't let you," he says.

"You were held back a grade, weren't you, Arnie?" Mom asks, but she continues on when Dad wrinkles his nose at a bad play. "How about no sleepovers until he has Bs?"

"No. We can't take away friends. He has few enough already."

"What else can we take away?" Mom clutches clumps of her graying hair and pulls.

"I get money for car sales. How about we give him money for good grades," Dad says.

7

Now we're talking.

"That is a bribe," Mom replies.

Suddenly, Dad leans toward the screen, jumps up, cheers, and pumps a fist when his team scores a touchdown. Mom hits power on the remote control, and Dad sits back down.

"Perhaps the environment is not conducive to maintaining attention," she says disapprovingly.

They are silent for a minute and then both burst out with the solution. Dad slaps his knee and my mom claps her hands.

"Bugs!" They shout and laugh and hug one another.

"We can't lose," my mother says. "Either he gets a B average or we take away all his creepy bugs."

"I love you," Dad says, holding Mom's pointy chin in his fingers. They start kissing.

Thankfully, I come to soon after.

"Not my bugs!" I shout at the ceiling fan.

"Jarrod? Are you all right?" my mother asks, leaning over me. "You've had a moment?" A moment. Syncope. A nightmare. I've been knocking my head on floors for a couple of years now, and doctors can't figure out why.

"No, I'm not okay. You're going to take away my bugs." I push myself up off the ground and brush cereal from my shoulder. "If it were baby animals I collected, no one would have a problem with it. Cute little baby foxes with little black noses—*oh, they're so cute*—but just because bugs have exoskeletons instead of fur, everyone hates them." I knock on my helmet as if my mother isn't only rejecting my bugs, but me as well.

My mom frowns, her lips thinning.

8

"I see you've talked with your father about your report card," she replies.

I am about to deny it, but then stop. As moments go, this has been a useful one for me, but how can I explain to her how I know she plans to take away my bugs? I can't even explain it to myself!

"We were planning to talk to you together . . ." She shakes her head. "Well, if your father shot off his mouth, then he can explain it to you. Go see him after classes today."

I nod. "But I want my bugs."

"How's your head?" she asks. "You don't want to miss your first day back at school."

"I'm fine, thanks to my stupid exoskeleton." I knuckle my helmet twice.

"That stupid helmet is keeping you from a concussion until we figure out what's wrong."

I might have preferred the concussion. When I first got the helmet, it had big eyes on it, but I painted over them in black. I didn't need any help sticking out.

"And, Jarrod, if you collected baby animals, we'd have even more of a problem. Even if they are cuter than bugs."

"Baby animals may be cute, but insects can be beautiful," I say, but she doesn't reply; she lifts her eyebrows and starts throwing documents into a briefcase.

"Go get your bag ready—you don't want to be late," she says finally.

I sigh and wander to my bedroom to make sure my bugs are safe. My parents are right. Science this summer was a breeze. I know all about insects, but what is so wrong with that? I am, however, terrified of being in a gifted class and wonder why Mr. Chang would do this to me. I am not smart. And definitely not gifted.

I peel the green tape from around my doorframe and quickly shut the door behind me. I keep a roll of green tape on a nail on both sides of the door, so I can seal it whether I'm coming or going. With four fresh strips, I secure the door once more.

In a corner of my ceiling, a cicada buzzes the alarm. *I've trained you well, my friend.* On the ceiling, the walls, the floors, even on my bed, everywhere crawl my bugs. They're my pets, my friends, pretty much all I really care about. And no way will I let my parents take them away.

Chapter 3
Where Jarrod's Mom Has a Thing

The cicada stops after I close the door. I like to think it's because it knows it's me. I shut my eyes and listen. First come the hissing cockroaches, and I put my tongue to the roof of my mouth and mimic. Soon after, the crickets begin to chirp. Most of my bugs—stinkbugs, walking sticks, praying mantises, rhinoceros beetles, harvester ants, and an African millipede longer than my foot—don't make any sound, or not sounds that I can hear. Humid air hangs in the perpetual twilight of my room. Just how the bugs and I like it.

I let the walking sticks and praying mantises climb everywhere. Mostly, my bugs skitter in their glass enclosures. They aren't allowed outside the room, hence the tape around the doorframe. Once, my dad found a praying mantis on his forehead when he woke up. It was probably trying to eat his brains. I can understand how that could freak you out. Ever since then, I have to tape. This suits me fine because it keeps the humidity in, and at night, my room smells, feels, and sounds like a tropical jungle.

I reach into the millipede enclosure and let Monkey coil

around my arm. I'm like the bug version of Snow White. Monkey's feet tickle, and she never bites. If ever she is frightened, Monkey rolls into a ball. Her black carapace is smooth to touch, and my fingers bump over the ribbed segments. I let her crawl back into her tank of peat moss and then slip her some of her favorite food: banana.

The cockroaches scuttle over each other in the terrarium. When I snap my fingers, all but one scurry about the edges of the glass tank and then stop in the middle.

"Cool," I say and place a sugar cube inside. I'd begun training them a couple of months ago and am surprised by how fast they learn but a bit dismayed that they forget almost as quickly. Bug brains just can't hold much for very long. I named one of the roachies Bent because its antennae are crooked. It's the one that doesn't move when I snap my fingers. Bent just stands there, but maybe it's the smartest of them all. Bent gets the sugar anyway and doesn't have to run around for it. Maybe it has evolved, but that's doubtful. Roachies haven't changed in three hundred million years—that's before the dinosaurs were around. You gotta respect that. If they had evolved, they'd probably be our bug overlords by now. Bent's probably just a little slow in the head. We've got a lot in common.

"How're my smart little roachies?" I coo and touch each on their exoskeletons. With my helmet, I feel a bit bug-like too. And our attention spans are about the same.

"First day of school," my mom shouts. "Wash your hands."

I draw another deep breath before untaping and retaping the door. This is not my first day of school. School never ended for me. I went to school all summer long, and here I go again.

My head itches, and I pull off the helmet to scratch my hair. Since wearing my helmet, I haven't had a haircut. Brown curls fall to my shoulders.

"You know you can't afford to do that," my mom says as she hands me my lunch. "Put it back on. I'm running late for work, and today's the day we're getting the settlement offer." She fits my helmet over my head and raps it into place. "Have a good day, love you."

She works at a law firm where she is trying for partner. That's her "thing," I guess. Her neat emerald skirt and white blouse remind me of a scarab beetle. I figure that's what she'd be if she were a bug. They're tough critters, and she's been fighting this court case against a giant drug company for three years.

I suspect I'd be a clown beetle. They fake death when threatened. My father is definitely a cockroach. And I don't mean that in a bad way. At least he isn't married to a praying mantis—they sometimes eat their husbands, but they're also the only insect that can turn their heads, which is so cool. Bugs with peripheral vision rock.

I watch my mother avoid all the cracks of the sidewalk. It must be a really important day if she's being superstitious like this. Then she hops on her electric scooter and hums off. I lock up the door and get on my bicycle, following after her. We live in a neighborhood with lots of houses squeezed in close to one another. The narrow streets have a grid pattern and are clogged with cars honking and screaming at one another, especially at this hour. School is only a couple miles away, but I need to be careful. Having a moment on a bike causes a lot of road rash. And my mom always orders me to take the sidewalk. Just in case.

I have thought a lot about my moments and what triggers them, and Gavin and I have debated what it could be. The moments come on suddenly. Sometimes I have a choking feeling or the sense of something caught in my throat. Most often it occurs while eating. For the longest time, the doctors thought it was an allergy to lettuce or fruit. Once I went strawberry picking and had three moments in a row before I gave up.

It is frustrating though. My condition means I can't swim without a life jacket, and even having a bath freaks my mom out, so she keeps checking on me. Biking is dangerous, and wearing a helmet all day in eighth grade? Well . . . that sucks. It's hard enough being the short kid who picks up bugs without sticking a helmet on top of it all.

But no amount of brain scans or psychotherapy has found anything. The best guess is that I have some strange form of epilepsy that no one can diagnose. Epilepsy is kinda scary, so I am holding out hope that my moments aren't grand mal seizures. There are no good treatment options, though. I have had four different trials of anti-seizure medications. The first three slowed me down and gave me even worse grades, and the last made me so hyper I never went to sleep and couldn't be touched without jumping. Each day's worth of medication was super expensive. In the mornings, my dad would hand me the pills and say, "Come on, son, chow down on another car sale."

After nothing worked, my doctor suggested I was making up my moments and said I should see a child psychiatrist. My mom keeps on saying it's probably some toxin from my bugs, but that doesn't make sense, does it? She's always looking for a reason to be rid of them for good.

My biking may be dangerous, but it is one of the few times I am like everyone else. At least, it's as close as I can get. I've fought hard for the right. It's freeing. It's completely normal.

I hear the ticking of a sprocket behind me, and I shake my head, knowing who is coming: Rick, the school bully.

Chapter 4
Where Bug-boy Meets the Dog-girl

"Bug-boy," Rick calls out. Rick's a big kid who has always been the bigger kid and who uses his bigness to shove people around and make himself feel even bigger. Weird thing is, Rick doesn't really need to do it. He's rich—mega rich—and it's his money, not his parents'. He was a child star as a baby, and his parents put everything he earned into Apple stock when it wasn't worth much. Now? It's worth millions. Money is Rick's *thing*. Wait—can money be a thing?

"Hey! Bug-boy!"

"Hiya, Richie Rich," I reply.

Since I started fainting, everyone—even Gavin—treats me differently, like I am about to keel over at any moment, which is technically true but still unlikely. Rick is an exception. He hasn't changed a bit. The only thing he's noticed is the stupid helmet. I appreciate that. Sort of.

"Bug-boy, if you ate a fruit fly, would that be like eating your sister?"

"I don't have a sister," I say.

"Whatever, but . . . like . . . would it?" Rick pedals at an easy pace. He could have a chauffeur. If I had his money, I'd design a special helmet that was cooler than not having one, like I could play video games with my mind, or something.

"How would I know if I don't have a sister?" I ask.

Rick just frowns and mutters something about bug brains.

"Rick?" I ask as he starts to bike ahead. "Is money your thing? What you want to be known for, I mean."

"No," he says, his face pinched and red. "You're an idiot." He accelerates away.

It pains me that I'm dumber than Rick, but maybe Gavin's right and I just need to find my amplitude or whatever he said. It's about focus, not brains.

I lock my bike up in the Hopewell Middle School bike racks. While I fiddle with the lock some first grader wanders up and says, "That's Bug-boy." And points me out to his mother like he's at a freak show and I'm an exhibit where the next attraction is the Strongman or the Bearded Lady.

Eighth graders are supposed to be at the top of the food chain. The lions of the school, the crocodiles, the T. rexes! But instead, I am a clown beetle. I have to figure out what is wrong with me so I can lose the helmet—without the helmet I won't be so recognizable. No one can see past the helmet. But I'm used to the teasing. I'm sort of like the roachie you try to squish. It keeps on walking.

"Don't worry," I say to the blushing mother. "I do like bugs. A lot." And I prove it by helping a fuzzy caterpillar off the walkway and to the leaf of a hibiscus bush.

She pulls her child away, and I climb the steps to the big double doors.

In addition to being my science teacher, Mr. Chang's also my homeroom teacher. He is the only person in class, setting up. A shock of white hair sticks up from his head that he constantly swipes at to smooth back. He waves as I enter. He already knows how my summer was. He was teaching me remedial science and now has sentenced me to gifted.

I'm here early as part of my promise to Gavin to play Monopoly. So, yeah, we're on the geek side of the spectrum, but even I don't like board games as much as he does—he takes forever to make decisions.

Playing board games has been a school tradition of ours since fourth grade. Each day last year we met a few minutes early to play. If I'm being honest though, it only became important to me after I started having my moments. Arriving early allows me to avoid the playground, the crowded hallways, people—I hate having moments in front of everyone. But this year Gavin and I only share two classes, homeroom and science. And I worry that the less time we spend together, the more likely I'll lose him as a friend.

This morning, I have a surprise for him. I've brought another cockroach with me, and this time I've trained it to stay put after it moves.

I slide my backpack onto the windowsill and pull out the board game to set it up while I wait. I always sit here, at the back corner of the class, because I'd rather not be around too many people. Roachie watches from his jar on my desk.

And that's when she sits down beside me. A tall girl with curly black hair. She has dimples and green eyes that are striking against her dark skin. A butterfly. A tailed jay butterfly.

"Graphium agamemnon," I whisper and wipe my palms on the Spiderman printed on my T-shirt. New-girl's dimples disappear.

"Are you speaking Greek?" she asks, dropping a backpack covered with badges from the Humane Society and other animal shelters. I shake my head, cursing my bug-brain and folding my hands on the desktop, hoping she'll ignore me. Her staring makes me want to vomit a little. This would not be the first time. Unfortunately, I have vomited on girls before. In fifth grade I must have eaten something nasty, because after lunch I spewed all down the front of Leanne Baron's dress. She moved away soon after. Not just to a different neighborhood, but right out of the country. This girl hasn't moved. She's waiting for an answer.

"I said: Gavin, I've got my game on." She squints at the Monopoly board and then back at me. "I was on my phone," I add. I don't have a phone.

If we were both standing and I barfed on New-girl, I would probably only hit her shorts, which are stained by muddy paw prints. By my estimate, the top of my helmet will reach New-girl's shoulder. Puberty can't hit soon enough.

Rick steps up beside her.

"You've met Bug-boy," he says to her.

Okay, so I know what to expect next. Rick will mock me. And New-girl may or may not appreciate it. It can really go either way. I try to think of myself as the bug watching from afar rather than as the topic of discussion.

Her eyes fall on Roachie climbing his jar, and her face twists into a look of such disgust that I wince. I gaze at the whiteboard where Chang preps notes. I'm like a male praying mantis and fully expect to have my head chewed off. I once wondered why the boy bugs don't fight while being eaten, but as I sit waiting to take it, I understand. They're terrified.

"Be careful where you walk. You might be squishing one of Bug-boy's relatives," Rick says. "One time there was a bee in the class, and the teacher went to kill it with his shoe and Bug-boy freaked out, dove, caught it in his hand and set it free out the window. Loser."

He's not waiting for a response from her. Rick has the floor and he's on a roll.

"What—are you like Dog-girl?" Rick laughs. Like I said, Rick doesn't really need friends. He has money for that, so he usually calls them as he sees them. I glance back at New-girl and see Rick picking at all the dog hair on her hoodie. Rick leans down and sniffs her. "Yup, Dog-girl." And he waves his hand before his nose and wanders off laughing.

We sit in silence for a moment before Dog-girl says, "I walk dogs."

"I like dogs," I say like an idiot.

There's another length of silence.

"You get stung?" she asks.

My brow pinches in confusion.

"From the bee you saved," she adds.

"Oh, no, male bumblebees don't sting. It was a boy."

"I like bees," she replies.

And of course, it's not the same thing as saying "I like bugs," but it's close enough. I swallow down the bit of bile that has climbed into my throat and grin behind my palm.

Chapter 5
Where Jarrod Is Gifted

"Do you have epilepsy?" Dog-girl asks, moving her head into my field of vision. "My little brother has to wear a helmet because he has epilepsy, at least until they get his seizures under control."

I'm pretty sure this is the longest conversation I've ever held with a member of the opposite sex—that isn't my mother or Gavin's older sister. I curse Gavin for being late and leaving me without a wingman.

"I don't know what I have," I say. "No one knows what I have."

"You mean you haven't Googled it?" she asks and laughs.

I don't want to talk about everything we've tried, and luckily Mr. Chang starts blathering away, and I can pretend I'm interested in that instead. Really, I inspect the bugs in the room. In one corner of the ceiling lives a little Parasteatoda tepidariorum, a common house spider. A zebra jumper hops across the teacher's desk, and a mosquito struggles in the web of a long-legged sac spider, which creeps slowly toward its lunch. By the end of class, I have no clue what Chang talked about, but I can tell you about any of the forty-six insects around me. A silverfish is even crawling right over Dog-girl's sneakers. I have learned not to point this out, as it always ends with screaming and stomping, so I stay quiet. Everyone deserves a chance, even bugs.

"What did your parents say about your report card, Jarrod?" Gavin asks, bouncing at my side. I shoot a look toward Dog-girl, but she's already packed up and is talking to the girl beside her.

Gavin really is practically a genius. By the age of two he could read and began trying to paint like the masters at age four. He still can't paint very well, but it sounds good when his parents brag about him.

"If I don't get Bs my parents will take away my bugs," I say.

"That bad, whoa." Gavin tucks his chin into his neck. He knows what it means for me to lose my bugs. "If my parents said they'd take away my dog, I'd be right mad. But I get As, all A pluses."

"Even P.E.?" I ask.

Gavin nods and does a little tap dance. Short, redheaded, Irish, and freckled, with bright keen eyes, Gavin gets teased for looking like a leprechaun, and the dancing doesn't help.

"You were too late for Monopoly," I say. And even as I say it, I realize how lame I sound.

"Sorry, how about after school?" he asks.

"Can't. Have to see my dad at the showroom after school," I say. "Tomorrow?"

"Maybe. Any more moments?" he asks.

"Big one this morning."

"Dog poop or maggots?"

Most of the time when I have my moments, I'm stuck staring

at dog poo or at maggots, rather than living rooms like the vision I had this morning. Gavin's asking which type I had. I am about to say neither, but this Monopoly business is really messing with my head. It was our thing, and he brushed it off. Instead of the truth, I say, "Both. Full-course meal."

"So gross." His cheeks billow out in a mock barf.

"Pretty much," I reply.

"Do you think maybe you've got a brain tumor?"

I roll my eyes. Despite Gavin knowing it's not a tumor, I still must say: "It's not a tumor." Because I admit that I'm frightened of what it could be. I *have* Googled it. It could be practically anything.

"Gotta run," he says. "Gifted."

All Gavin's other classes are in the Gifted stream, so I won't see much of him except at recess, morning homerooms, and science class for as long as it takes for Chang to realize he made a mistake and kick me out. Dog-girl doesn't seem to have any of my classes either, and so I go from Math to Social Studies to English and French all while studying the various species of bugs in each room. In Social Studies, I jump up and point out the window.

"Assassin bug!" I shout.

The teacher stops. "Pardon me?"

"So cool—bloodsucking Assassin bug. Sometimes they're called kissing bugs because they bite people around the mouth."

"Ewwww," goes the class.

"They have a powerful venom that liquefies the inside of the bugs they eat so they can suck it out through their rostrum, which is sort of like a straw."

"Ewwww!"

The insect crawling on the tree branch is black-brown, about the size of my pinky finger, with a long neck and smallish wings.

"Sit, Jarrod. We are discussing the current issues facing the Middle East. How about sharing your thoughts on that topic?" The teacher's hand chops in my direction.

I keep staring at the bug until she moves on. Most of the teachers are used to me or have heard about me, but they forget sometimes—they need retraining, a little like my roachies. Mr. Chang, however, isn't quite so easy to push over.

"Jarrod!" he calls on me during science class. No one put up their hand to outline the human body's digestive system. "Tell us about your guts."

I shrug and hunker into my seat. *I'm so gutless.* He pulls at his hair so it's all tufted out like he's got a head of dandelion fluff.

"You know it. You just don't realize you do. Tell us about a bug's internal systems."

I swallow.

"Well, they've got a mouth, right?" I ask.

"Good, yes, yes, and . . ." He twirls his hand around and returns to the whiteboard to draw a mouth.

"There are these glands that produce saliva and an esophagus. A bug's stomach is more like a tube, and then there are some bottom parts."

He draws all this but stops at the stomach.

"Bottom parts? This is science class. Names, please." He taps the board with the marker.

"You know, intestines, rectum . . . anus," I whisper the last.

The class muffles their laughter.

"Excellent," he cheers. "And I believe you'll find, Jarrod, that the circulatory system and nervous system are similar too."

I blink. "Even the brain?"

"Especially the brain."

He moves on to grill other students, but for the first time I wonder if I actually am in the right class. Then he begins talking about stuff requiring numbers, and my eyes glaze over.

After school, I bike to the car dealership where my dad works—in an industrial park. The dealership sells Fords. Without a sidewalk, I stick to the gravel shoulder of the road. Sunlight reflects from the windshields of a hundred cars and trucks and acts like a beacon. I don't bother locking up my bike when I get there. I leave it near the back and then walk around to the showroom.

"Hi, Jarrod, love the lid," says the receptionist. He is this super muscular guy with a tattoo of a spider on his arm. I haven't worked up the nerve to tell him that it's missing a couple of legs.

"Thanks. You see my dad?" I ask.

He jabs a thumb over his shoulder. My dad is on the floor with a couple who are dressed like they're Ferrari shopping but are inspecting the lowest end of Ford's car lineup. The woman has her arms folded across her chest, but the guy is listening intently to my father.

My dad has a bit of a gut, but his suit jacket hides it pretty well. My mom is always telling him he needs to lose the belly fat, but Dad is on his feet all day and likes to put them up when he's at home. That's what he says.

He has this broad, trustworthy face and a million-watt smile. He isn't smiling right now, and I can tell by the sweat beaded on his brow that today has not been a good day.

Chapter 6
Where Jarrod Sells a Car

Seeing me, my dad pats the man on the shoulder, frowns at the woman, and then gives me a dim smile as he approaches.

"Hey, Jarrod, how's m'boy?"

"Mom says you're going to take away my bugs if I don't get Bs." I have decided that the best way to bring up the issue is for him to think Mom told me.

His face darkens. "We were supposed to talk to you about this together. Listen, I've got a tough sell over there." The couple has migrated to the water cooler and sip from paper cones as they argue. "Give me ten minutes, and we'll talk about it."

He pats me the same way he patted the customer and then pops the hood on a car model, which, by my dad's own admission, is little more than a lawnmower with bigger wheels. The prospective customers seem much more animated and leave the cooler to join my father.

Thirsty from my bike ride, I take their place at the cooler and fill a cup. I chug it back.

Then I hit the floor.

It's my second moment today—another good one. Once

again, I'm not on the floor looking up; it's like I'm at the water cooler and looking out toward the couple.

"I am not going to be caught driving around in this." The woman's talking. I am unable to look away from her or the guy, who has one finger pressed to his temple.

How the heck am I seeing their discussion? Nothing makes sense, but I have no choice except to listen.

"Why not? It's a perfectly good car," he says. "Are you afraid of what people will think?" I watch her swallow, and the guy slaps his forehead. "You are! So that's what this is all about. Do you really think having a sporty car will change anything for you?"

"I am in sales, and I need to at least look like I'm good at it. That's a soccer mom car."

"It's a good value," he says. "And what's wrong with being a soccer mom? I want to be a soccer dad."

She flushes a deep shade of red and scratches her nails over her arm, leaving long welts. I think she's going to explode, but instead she hisses through her clenched teeth. "You can buy that car. I will buy another car, something with a powerful engine, fire-engine red, and an awesome stereo system. Then we'll be paying for two leases instead of one."

"We can't afford a sports car."

"I'll sell more. I'll skip vacations."

What's weird is that, instead of the guy getting all upset, a grin spreads across his face. "It's a deal. Let's blow out of here," he says.

"Yeah." Her eyes light up.

When I snap out of it, my dad is hovering over me.

"Moment?" he asks.

"Dad, stop those people from leaving." I waggle my hand.

"They're not . . ." he begins, but his face droops when he glances over to see them pushing through the doors into the parking lot. "Why are they leaving?"

"They don't want a lawnmower; they want something flashier. Hurry." I grip his shoulder as if I'm telling him a desperate secret.

"Upsell, eh? How do you know?" His brow's furrowed in confusion.

"Go—before they leave, get them to look at something fast, and don't forget to tell them it comes in fire-engine red!"

He slaps his leg. "Well, I've got nothing to lose. You sure you're okay?"

I nod and give him a big thumbs-up. For once, I feel like my moments might not be all bad.

Twenty minutes later, my dad's smile goes thermonuclear as he returns to where I sit waiting on a couch. I'm pretty sure I just helped my dad sell a car.

"How'd you know, Jarrod?" His arm is draped over my shoulder, and I am feeling proud of myself. Through the windows I watch the couple drive out in a car twice the price of the ones my dad had been showing them.

I wonder if I should tell him about my moments. I've tried before, but they keep calling them auditory and visual hallucinations, which lead to more visits with doctors. I don't enjoy doctors. No, I can't tell him.

"A hunch, I guess," I explain. "I mean, she had her arms crossed the whole time and . . . and kept on looking at the faster cars."

"Geez, you even knew the color she wanted. Well, you can be a fly on the wall for me anytime." This time he squeezes my shoulder. I haven't felt so close to him in a while. I lean my head onto his arm. "Maybe we could be a team?" He laughs.

"Speaking of flies," I say, "does this mean I can keep my bugs?"

The arm around my shoulder drops, and he twists to look me in the eyes. "You need to improve your grades, Jarrod. What did you learn today in school?"

"I saw an Assassin bug, *and* I identified a cicada in its larval stage. I wonder if we're going to have an infestation this year."

"You identified a maggot?"

"Well, I think they prefer to be called larvae. Maggot might be offensive, but you never really know what bugs a bug. Although I *can* tell when the roachies are happy." My dad has this crazed look on his face. "Look, Dad, I know you're worried about jobs, but I can be a scientist."

"Grades, Jarrod. To be a scientist you need good grades. Plural."

"But—"

"We'll talk later, Jarrod. I think I'm on a roll. And you need to crack those books."

He nudges me to the side as a woman walks onto the showroom floor and inspects a black pickup truck. His smile dials brighter and his spine straightens. Selling cars is my dad's thing.

I slink off the couch and leave without saying goodbye.

Chapter 7
Where Jarrod Swallows a Fly

Eight. That's my record for the number of moments in one day. It happened a year ago. I was on a father-son camping trip at a massive campground where no one can sleep at night because of all the noise. We had only been there an hour when I had my first moment. My dad was frazzled because we were swimming and he had to pull me onto the beach before I regained consciousness.

"Boy, would your mom be angry if you drowned," he says. "She even *said* no swimming."

I had a second moment walking back to the campsite. I don't remember much from that trip, but what I really remember are all the bugs: mosquitoes, black flies, deer flies, gnats, and horseflies. We joked later about it having been the only time we could agree that bugs can be bad. And if it hadn't been for all the moments, the bugs alone might have driven us home. Ants had found our food, and we ate lunch picking them out of our baked beans. That meal included two more moments.

After lunch, we went to the tent and lay down for a nap, and it was weird because I woke up having yet another moment. I never even told my dad about that one. The last straw was when we were hiking and I almost fell over a cliff. That might have just been me tripping, but my dad didn't care. It had been a rough day. We packed up soon after and haven't gone camping since.

Usually though, several days go by between moments, and I don't worry too much about them. Having two in the same day begs some analysis. I go over them in my mind as I bike home. Both moments were while eating or drinking, and if I think about it, a lot of my moments happen then. But that isn't news, and I've been checked out for every allergy imaginable. I am a bit allergic to things like dust and mold, but no foods—although I'd been hoping for broccoli. How could I have an allergy to drinking water? None of it made sense.

Out of the industrial park, I pedal along the sidewalks of our little main street. We live in a neighborhood that is part of a much larger city. The sidewalk's crowded now and people yell at me for biking on it, but I don't bother to stop and explain that my mom makes me. I am too busy thinking. I'm sure that I'm on to something.

I turn down Mapleview, heading home, when something flies into my mouth and lodges in the back of my throat. I make a choking sound, realize that I am not going to hack whatever it is out, and decide that the only possible course of action is to swallow it as quickly as possible. I wobble, jerking the handlebars left and right. I aim for a patch of freshly mown grass.

And then I'm somewhere else.

Dog poop moments are the worst. So many moments start out up close and personal with a nugget of poo, and most end that way. And let me tell you: up this close, it magnifies the smell

31

at least a billion times. Sometimes I hop from one nugget to another as if trying to find *the* best poo. This time it isn't a nugget, rather a soft puddle. A blur of green surrounds me. Then I catch another whiff of something.

To me, this new smell is a billion times worse than poo. I know the reek but can't place it. I will find out soon enough, however. I cover the distance close to the ground, so my landmarks are lawns, concrete curbs, sidewalks covered in chalk drawings, a garbage can—whoa—I get stuck at the garbage can and play with some maggots—larvae are my second worst moments. Overwhelming the garbage smell comes the acrid stench of burning tires. This whole vision is a doozy. A bell rings and then I hear something creepy.

Creak, creak, Creak, creak. The sound scratches at my ears. It's a sound from a horror movie. The wind blows the rotting smell back my way and drags me from my larvae buddies, over a paved driveway to bump into someone's basement window.

Somehow, I manage to slip past the glass even though the window isn't open. Inside the basement, I am winging down a wood-paneled wall. Light struggles through the grimy window behind me. But I can still see well enough, and now the location of the smell is obvious. A large box is in the center of the room. The top of the box almost reaches to the ceiling and has a steel door in one of its heavily padded sides.

As moments go, this is already a long one, and it's also the first time I've been terrified. Nothing good can be rotting in a box in a basement. I don't want to see what's inside.

Wake up, I urge myself, but I know it's not possible. Fear has wrapped its talons around my throat.

Helplessly, I flit over wall-to-wall lime green shag carpeting. A couch is pushed up beside a lava lamp within which bubbles of hot wax float. But whatever is causing my moment isn't all that interested in the basement decor. It wants the surprise inside the box.

I recognize where I have encountered this stink. Roadkill. Now I really don't want to see what is in this box.

I knock up against the cold steel door and then swoop down to pause at the very bottom. A thin crack of light shines from beneath, and I move forward, passing under the door into the box.

I navigate a forest of shag carpeting, and then the floor turns into linoleum. I launch into the light to survey the small room. Cages stacked four high line every inch of wall space. The whines, yips, and barks of the dogs inside overwhelm me. I want to put my hands over my ears, but of course, I can't. Worse than the noise, however, is the smell. Urine, feces, and the sweet roadkill scent.

Wet noses press against the cages, little black noses attached to clouds of fur. Puppies, dozens of puppies. I circle and soon see that other dogs are in the cages too. Adult dogs—the mommy dogs. Some stare out longingly. One struggles to lift its head, a yellow crust sealing its eyes. White spittle drools from its mouth before it collapses. Others lie on their sides, letting puppies suckle for milk. I watch their too-quick breaths and see their bony ribs sticking far out. These dogs aren't just sick, underfed, unexercised, and uncared for—they're dying. And then I'm through the bars of another cage.

In it lies a dog all alone. Her fur is matted and tangled. Froth bubbles around her muzzle as she labors for breath. The distended belly tells me she's fat with puppies. But she's also very, very sick.

The smell is coming from her hip. Flies buzz and hop around an open sore that weeps yellow ooze. The flies cloud the air after a swipe of the dog's tail. The poor girl barely has room to stand in the cage, let alone move around. The sore must be from lying on one side day in and day out. This is the type of moment where I really wish I had eyes to close, but I can't look away.

To my horror, I move closer still, until I am walking through the gooey mess of her hip. I stare down suckling flies. Flies taste with their feet. They're tasting her. *Double gross.* Then, sensing movement, I take off as the dog's tail swats again. Another flail sends me back through the cage and under the door, and into the basement. I want to race back, to open the cages and free the poor creatures, but I can't stop my vision. I backtrack and go out through the window to forage for more poop and have more maggot playdates. *Creak, creak* . . . go the creepy sounds, and the stench of tar dissipates as the world blurs.

And then I am clutching grass, half off my bike, lying on my side a little like the poor dogs.

"Are you all right?" a woman asks. She's pushed a stroller with four two-year-olds up onto the lawn beside me. She has dark circles under her eyes.

"Yes, sure, yeah." I struggle to process what I saw. "I fell off my bike. I'm fine."

I look left and right, but there isn't a window around like the one I went through. Just my regular neighborhood. A crow caws, and a motorcycle rumbles down the main street. I think back to what happened just before the start of the moment. It's important. The reason for my moments is on the tip of my tongue.

One of the kids starts to cry, waking up another. The woman gives me another long look before pushing her charges back onto the sidewalk.

I stop breathing for a second.

I finally understand.

The reason for my moments isn't on the tip of my tongue; it's in the back of my throat. I think I know what's happening to me.

And it's crazy.

Chapter 8
Where Jarrod Forms a Hypothesis

I pedal over to Gavin's house and knock on the door. His sister answers.

"Gavin, Bug-boy's here," she calls and then walks away, leaving the door open.

Gavin hops down the stairs to the landing and freezes. "What's wrong?"

"Just come with me," I say.

To my relief, Gavin grabs a jacket and a bike helmet of his own from the closet, yelling: "Tell Mom I'm going out with Jarrod."

A good friend will come with you as soon as you ask.

There's no answer to Gavin's call, but he shuts the door behind him. Gavin, being Gavin, doesn't remain quiet for long. "So, where are we going? What's happening? Why are you totally pale?"

"I think I know what's causing my moments. I want to test it." I hop back on my bike. "Follow me."

I'm silent the rest of the ride, and even though I'm not replying, he keeps on guessing, knowing that if he guesses right I'll give some sign.

"Bright flashing lights do it? No, maybe dehydration—how much water do you drink a day? Heart condition. Low blood pressure. Panic attacks. Wait, you're taking drugs? You're going to show me the crack house where you deal!"

I shake my head.

A river runs through our city, and during the summer I often go down to the bike path that follows it and bushwhack for a bit until I reach the riverbank. I'm not the only one. A lot of homeless people camp out along the river. If I disturb them, I move on and find my own cool place to squat. Sometimes the birdsong is so loud that it overwhelms the traffic noises, making me feel like I could be in the middle of the wilderness. And, of course, there are the bugs.

This summer, I found the perfect spot to lounge: in the well of three cottonwood tree trunks, their bark ropey and cracked, their branches stretched akimbo.

There I leaned back against one trunk and put my legs on a second, as great tufts of their seeds fell like snow all around me. Frogs croaked for mates. Water striders skated over the ponderous river surface. I floated with the broad-leaved arrowhead lilies that rested beside rose, white, and red flowers. But today I'm not looking for tranquility. Today I want privacy and bugs. It takes ten minutes to reach the spot on the river trail.

The whole time I biked, I kept my lips pressed together. I breathe heavily through my nostrils now as I struggle to push my bike through the undergrowth and carry it over fallen logs. Gavin crashes along behind me. Finally, with sweat pouring down both our faces, we find the trees at the edge of the river.

"All right, are you going to tell me what we're doing here?"

Gavin asks as he pulls his bike up beside mine.

I glance left and right, but no one lurks in the trees nor paddles the river. I lean my bike against a trunk and climb up into its embrace.

"You ready?" I ask.

Gavin sits on the ground and stares at me. "I'm here, aren't I?"

"This is what I think: When I eat bugs, I black out and I see and hear and smell what they saw, heard, and smelled before I ate them."

I've never seen Gavin give the kind of blank stare he's giving me now.

"I don't understand," he says.

"If I eat a bug, I pass out or something, but only for however long the bug has a memory. Sometimes the memory isn't long, and that makes sense given how quickly roachies forget their training, right? I mean, how much can a fruit fly remember?"

"What makes sense? This doesn't make sense," he says. "You can't be serious?"

"I know," I say, holding up my hands because I can tell he wants to leave. "This is my best guess. It explains why so many moments include dog poo. It explains why it happens more during camping, swimming in a lake, and eating. I don't really like to think that I've swallowed quite so many bugs, but listen, an hour ago I was biking, swallowed a fly, and then had a moment. It was a really clear moment that took me places only a fly could go and to a place only a fly would want to go."

Gavin leans forward and says, "You should talk to your therapist about this, or maybe it's a side effect of a drug. Are you taking something new?"

"No, Gavin. I'm sure of this."

"But it's not possible," he says.

"Isn't this what science is about?" I ask. "Answering questions like this? Deciding if it is possible or not? I only have to test the theory. I need to eat a bug. On purpose."

"You want to eat an insect?" He laughs. "The kid who cried when we went fishing and my dad showed him a collection of his flies? They weren't even real flies!"

"Of course I don't want to eat a bug. Bugs are cool, not tasty. But do you have a better idea? How else can I test it?" I ask, hoping Gavin might have an answer.

Gavin looks like he's about to say something then stops, then starts again, then stops and then starts talking to himself. "What's the worst can happen, Gavin? So he eats a bug. Whatever." Finally, he throws up his hands. "All right. If you're going to do this, let's do it right."

I smile. It's another thing I love about Gav. He can let stuff slide. "Thanks, Gavin. Let me find a bug."

I glance around. How should I choose a bug to eat? Do I go on the basis of size? Expected taste? Do I want to eat an ant? Will it only work with flies? Considering the ants in the beans episode, I guess it works for all sorts of bugs.

Gavin's right, though. How can I eat a bug? I love bugs! But I need to figure this out. It's important. This could be the answer to what is wrong with me, and I might be able to stop future moments. I steel myself. Gavin starts to whistle the "Ants Go Marching" song.

I try to catch a fly, but it keeps evading me, flitting through my cupped hands to perch a few feet away. After a couple minutes, I decide to pick something slower. A mosquito lands on my forearm. I let it bite down while I decide if it is to be my dinner. Then I think about how it could have sucked something's—or someone else's—blood already, and that would make it gross to eat.

Grosser. Although it would be a righteous act. Mosquitoes have killed more people than all the wars combined. Forget world peace—eradicating mosquitoes is more important.

I check under a rock and decide that potato bugs won't actually taste like potatoes, and besides, they're actually crustaceans that can drink from their own butts—seriously awesome. A beetle climbs the bark of the tree, but that is way too big. I don't want anything I have to chew. I don't really like the idea of killing a bug at all.

But I also know that people all around the world eat bugs. Mealworms, grasshoppers, dung beetles, wasps, locusts, termites, stinkbugs, and . . . ants. The ants are everywhere here.

"Okay," I say, coming back to the ants. "I know what I'm going to eat, but I want to give him a last meal." From my backpack, I draw out my lunch box, where a few scraps linger from my sandwich. I hope to give my little friend a couple minutes alone with the crumbs. With the edge of the container tilted onto the bark, a little red ant marches along the rim and then inside.

"Thanks, buddy," I say. "I promise you won't feel a thing."

Chapter 9
Where Jarrod Is Not a Plonker

"Wait. Don't kill the ant yet," Gavin says. "Give it here."

I hand Gavin the container with the ant inside. Without another word, he pushes off into the brush.

"Can you see me?" he shouts.

"No!" I reply.

A few seconds later, Gavin returns, bare legs scratched by thorns.

"What did you do?" I ask.

"I'm not telling, but eat it quick before the memory fades . . ." Gavin rolls his eyes. "I did not just say that. Get this over with."

I hover my finger above the little guy. Ants can live as long as fifteen years. One type even farms their own food. In aggregate, they outweigh humanity many times over. I'm just some thirteen-year-old kid, not an executioner.

"I hope you've had a good life," I say and then squish it with my fingertip. It crunches a little and its head separates from its thorax. "Told you it wouldn't take long." I hope it didn't hurt too much. If a giant decapitated me, I probably wouldn't feel it.

I eye the little smear.

"I wish I had some ketchup," I say.

"I have a mint for after."

"Did you know that some termites taste minty?"

"Are you going to eat it, or what?"

I've had scores of moments—why can't I just lick it and be done with it? Maybe I can. Maybe I'm thinking too much.

In a single motion, I bring the container to my mouth and lick the ant. I feel it between my teeth, gag a little, and then swallow.

Nothing happens.

I sag back against the tree.

"I knew it," Gavin says. "I can't believe you did that. But I knew it wouldn't work. Maybe it *is* all in your head."

I was so sure. And now I've eaten an ant for nothing. I am about to shove the container into my knapsack when I realize I haven't eaten the ant. Not the entire ant.

"Wait, the head, you're right. Maybe it's because I missed its head," I say. Gavin's already at his bike and he sighs, gripping the handlebars, but waiting.

I squint down at the ant head. Somehow knowing I was prepared to eat the whole ant all at once doesn't help me eat just its head—its brains! I sigh and lick again.

And fall out of the tree.

Did it work? I stare back at myself, but my vision is partially obscured by a boulder of food. It does work! I *am* the ant.

Then the entire world is a blur, and I hear the crashing of trees as if some dinosaur tromps down the forest.

"Can you see me?" Gavin shouts, and I hear myself shout back.

Then Gavin's face looms before me. "Jarrod is a plonker. Jarrod is a plonker." He holds up three fingers and the world blurs again and I hear crashing noises. In comes a giant fingertip. It presses down, and I see the glow of sunlight through the fleshy bits of the fingertip as it squishes. There's a terrible crunch. And then the body is separated, and still I look on until finally everything begins to dim and a great tongue is lolling down. So, it didn't die quite as quickly as I had thought. *Sorry, ant!*

I come around, staring at the river. Gavin's confused face looms right above me.

"It's a coincidence," he says.

I jerk forward, causing Gavin to stumble backward.

"*Whoop!* Oh, yeah, baby!" Not only do I not have epilepsy, I have a superpower—not the best or tastiest superpower, sure, but still a real superpower. I can't believe it. I'd begun to believe the doctors who said that I was faking it. I'm not sick. I'm better than not sick! It's like a crushing weight has lifted from my chest. Everything makes sense. Why else would I love bugs so much?

"What did I say?" Gavin challenges. He's crawled forward to kneel at my side, eyes confused and looking right at me.

"I am not a plonker. I am *not* a plonker." And then I hold up three fingers, not even caring what a plonker means.

Gavin's eyes widen.

"I am not a plonker! I am . . ." I stop, thinking hard. This is the moment of truth for all superheroes, when they accept their super identity. "I am Bug-boy!"

I can't believe I gave myself Rick's name for me. But maybe the name makes sense. I'll own it now. Let him call me Bug-boy.

For once, Gavin is at a loss for words.

Chapter 10
Where Jarrod Tells the World

"I have *so* many questions," Gavin says after he recovers. "How does it work? Do you really think you're accessing the bug's brain?"

"I don't know," I say. "I—"

"Do you see what it sees? I mean, like an ant? What does an ant see? Does it use echolocation or something?"

"You're thinking of bats; ants have terrible vision," I say.

"See what I mean? How could you have seen the fingers? What are you tapping into then? Is this some weird fluke? Something completely different than what we think?"

He's pulling at his bush of red hair.

"I don't need more experiments, Gav. I've used it to help my dad at work. It explains everything."

He stares at me and then picks up a big beetle that's climbing up a tree and starts moving toward me. "Here—"

"No way." I pick up my bike and plow back through the brush while he calls after me. "Later!" I shout. For now, I need to talk to my mom and dad. It's not just to tell them the amazing news. It's because I need help.

If I am seeing the last few minutes of a bug's life, then everything I've seen is real. And that means dogs are really and truly trapped in a basement somewhere. I've decided that it's a puppy mill. Someone is making money selling puppies from sick mommy dogs without any care for how the dogs are treated, forcing the mother dogs to pump out puppies until they're dead. Maybe the puppy mill is nearby, maybe not. But I can't think of my moments as dreams any longer. Or near-death experiences. Or some view of the future. They are real. Just then an image seizes me of the poor dog trying to lift its head, blind and defeated.

I need to act.

"Mom!" I yell as I push through the front door, but of course, she isn't home yet. No one is here except me and my bugs. I shut the door. The hall is cool and quiet, and I feel very alone. Someone, perhaps someone on my own street, is not a very nice person. I can't wait for my mom; I have to do something. *I* certainly can't help the dogs. But I can't let my nerves be the reason why the dogs remain trapped either. I have to call the police.

I stride through the hall and pick up the kitchen phone. I hesitate for a few seconds before dialing 911.

"9-1-1, do you require police, fire, or ambulance?" the dispatcher asks.

"Police," I say to the query, my heart thudding so hard against my ribs that it hurts.

"What's the nature of your emergency?" she continues.

"Someone's running a puppy mill, and the dogs are really sick and need help," I say. My feet dance beneath me. I can't seem to hold still.

"Where is the location?" the operator asks.

"I don't know. I've only seen all the puppies and the dogs—they can't stand, one's eyes are all gooped up, and another has this terrible sore on her," I explain.

"What's the name of the puppy mill owner?"

I frown into the handset.

"I . . . I don't know that either, only . . ." My toes stop their tapping and I lean my forehead against the wall, guessing the next question. This isn't working. She probably thinks I'm joking.

"Go ahead, what can you tell me?" At this point, the dispatcher is still being all professional and urgent.

"They are in a basement, trapped in a room. The basement has thick carpet and wooden walls. There's a lava lamp." My voice is getting higher. "You know, one of those lights with gloop inside that moves around?"

"What's the address?" I catch the hint of impatience in her voice.

"I don't know," I squeak out. "They're all in cages in a big box in a room."

"You're saying that there is a puppy mill in a box, in a wooden room, but you can't tell me where it is?"

There is a pause.

"What's your name, dear?" This isn't about the dogs anymore. This is about me.

"Jarrod Belanger. Listen, I know it sounds like a prank, but it's not."

The dispatcher sighs.

"Where did you see the dogs? Where is the basement? The room?"

"I don't know." I feel like I'm being wrung out.

"Then how did you see it?"

"I . . . I swallowed a fly," I blurt. "I think it was a fly, definitely bigger than a mosquito because I choked on it a bit, and I met other flies. If I eat bugs, I see what they see. Saw."

"If you eat bugs, you can see what they see-saw?"

"Saw, like what they remember. Yes. I eat them, then I fall down, and it's like a vision. I tested it."

I'm holding my forehead with one hand, and the handset is pressed so tight to my ear that it hurts.

"Jarrod, is there a parent home? An adult I can speak to?"

"No, I'm alone."

"How old are you? Do your parents know you're alone?"

"I'm thirteen, they know! It's not illegal."

"Jarrod, false calls to 911 operators are criminal offenses. It uses time and resources that could be going to true emergencies."

"I know . . . I know. But this is an emergency. You have to believe me." Tears of frustration spring to my eyes.

"Do you have anything—any evidence—that could help me believe you?" she asks. There's compassion in her voice that only makes it worse.

I shake my head, but she can't see me.

"Jarrod?"

"No, ma'am. I have nothing."

"I will be filing a report on your call, Jarrod. I have your location, number, and name. If you proceed to make more false calls, this one will also count against you."

I hang my head. I have nothing left. "Yes, ma'am."

"Jarrod?" I turn to see my mom standing in the entry to the kitchen.

47

The phone slips to my chest.

"Who are you talking to?" she asks.

I hang up on the 911 operator.

My mom twists the rings on her fingers. She does this when she's stressed. I hope she isn't stressed about me.

"What is it? It sounded like you were talking to the police," she says.

"If I tell you something, do you promise to believe me?" I ask.

"I can't promise anything until I hear what you want me to believe," she says.

"I know what causes my moments," I say.

"Go on." She squints.

"It's when I swallow bugs."

"You think it's their toxins," she says, and her shoulders sag a little. She stops twisting her rings. Maybe she thought I had really bad news. Like I'm expelled from school. "I wonder how we can test that. If eating bugs makes this happen, we need to get rid of all the bugs in the house. We'll hire an exterminator."

I draw a deep breath. "I have tested it, but it's not their toxins. My moments are their bug memories."

Her shoulders draw back up, and she starts spinning her rings again.

"I don't understand, honey," she says quietly, and I hear the fear in her voice. Suddenly I feel like she's tiptoeing around me. Like I'm a bomb that could go off at any moment. She's always on the lookout for a reason for my moments. To find and fix what is obviously wrong with my brain.

Some doctors have suggested that my moments are all in my head, meaning I somehow make them happen. It's why the police dispatcher asked for an adult—she thought I'm going nuts. Wait. *What if I am?* No, I proved it to Gavin. I can prove it again.

After a deep breath, I explain. "You know how I knew about how you were going to take away my bugs if I didn't get better grades?"

She nods. "Your father."

"No, actually, Dad hadn't told me. I'd seen it during a moment. I must have eaten a bug that had watched you. And this afternoon I ate a bug at a water cooler and helped Dad sell a car with it. And then on the way home I choked down a fly and saw a bunch of dogs abused in a basement . . ."

My mom steps forward and gathers me into her arms. She starts sobbing. "Oh, honey, honey, we'll figure it out. We will, I promise. I know it's hard."

I don't understand for a second and then push her away by the shoulders. "No, I'm serious. This is all true. It all happened!"

She composes herself. Wipes her eyes. Takes a couple breaths, and then responds: "I understand that you *think* it's true—"

"It is!" I scream. "I can prove it. Find me a bug, a fly, an ant, anything." My head whipsaws searching, but the one time I really need a bug, they've deserted me. "I'll sacrifice one of my own even, and then you say something in this room with me outside and then I'll eat it and tell you what you said . . ."

"No." My mom is firm. "That is crazy, and I will do no such thing."

"I know it's crazy, but I'm not!"

"I will not be talked to like this." She's pulling at her rings so hard, I'm worried she'll tear a finger off.

I start shaking. My hands are clenched into fists.

"I thought you'd be happy that I figured it out. I solved it."

"What will make me happy is if you start buckling down to your homework. If you applied as much creativity to your English class, maybe you wouldn't need to resort to these stories in order to keep your bugs!"

I squint at her. She thinks I'm telling her all this to save my bugs?

She turns away and pulls out her phone to stare at it.

"I'm putting the finishing touches on the settlement. Not as much as I had wanted, but close," she starts babbling about work, and I can tell that she's going to crack if I push any harder. "I am going to bring you to the office with me tomorrow. We'll pretend it's bring your kid to work day. It would be nice for you to see where an education can take you." She points to her calendar on her phone and smiles at me as if we'd just been talking about what to have for dinner.

"No," I say. "I don't want to be a lawyer."

Her smile thins. "That was not a suggestion, Jarrod," she replies. "You're sick. I want you where I know you are safe. You're coming." She spins on her heel to stomp into her bedroom, where she shuts the door. I think of the dogs locked up. Locked up. *Forever.*

I am alone in this. If the police won't help, if my mother won't believe me, I'll have to help the dogs. Somehow.

Chapter 11
Where Jarrod Trains His Army

I seal the door to my bedroom with green tape and sag against it. I need help—someone who will trust me without asking too many questions. Is that too much to ask? Gavin's the only one I can think of. I check my email. Sure enough, Gavin's recovered from the shock of our discovery and has sent me a message.

Okay, so I've racked my brain, and I don't know how you could have known what I said to the ant. Or how many fingers I showed the ant. Fingers—ant. Do you realize how bonkers this is? So impossible. But I guess what I'm trying to say is that I believe you. Mostly. Pretty much. There are more tests I'd like to run. A battery of experiments under six conditions, which we'll then need to repeat with different bugs at various stages of development. After that, I'll totally believe you . . .

He goes on, but I don't read it and don't reply. I don't need to run more tests. It is good to know Gavin's got my back though—sort of—especially after my conversation with my mom, and especially because I thought I might be losing my friend.

I sneak out of the house. Maybe I'll recognize something

from my moment that will lead me to the basement with the dogs. Back on my bike, I slowly crisscross the streets in a grid search. I try to imagine myself as a fly. I search out dog poo and garbage. But there's plenty of that, especially when you're looking for it. I keep my ears cocked for the creaky, horror movie sound, and I slow to sniff the air for tar, but nothing.

A girl stares at me from her porch when I stop at the end of her walkway to look more closely at a big poo pile. But it's not a pile I know personally. Would the owners of the puppy mill have more dog poo on their lawn than others? Not if they never let the dogs out.

I shudder and pedal on. Three streets over I catch sight of a chalk drawing on the sidewalk and rush to it. The drawing is of a house and a tree with a swing. In one corner is a big sun with lots of rays of sunlight poking off it, and a cloud is in the other corner. I shut my eyes and try to think back to the chalk drawings I'd passed in the moment, but I don't remember any one in particular. My memory isn't much better than a bug's.

I study the nearby houses. These are single-story homes with nice gardens out front and narrow driveways. Some driveways are paved, others cobblestone. I don't remember any cobblestone from the vision or the big planters in front of another house. This is tough. A man walks by straining to hold back a German shepherd. Would the bad guys be regular dog owners? I don't know. If I liked dogs, I'm not sure I could hurt them. I don't pull wings off flies. *No, you just eat them.*

I bike on and find three more chalk drawings before clouds gather and the first spackles of rain hit the pavement. Soon the chalk drawing evidence will be gone.

The range of a housefly is up to five miles, so that gives me a search area of five miles in every direction, which is pretty much the entire city. At least I didn't swallow a dragonfly. Those suckers can fly fifty miles per hour. But I can't search the city, not alone. Not even with Gavin's help. Even if I could, I'd have to watch for a while in every area to pick up clues. I need a better method. As rain begins to fall, I sit down on the curb and consider the resources available.

In front of me, a fuzzy caterpillar dangles from a thread of silk. As I watch, it slips to the pavement. A whole host of them have been squished by passing cars. I'm not alone, I realize. I have bugs!

For me, bugs are like having cameras on every block. Not very good cameras, mind you, but still, so many! What else can I do with bugs? Maybe if I find something suspicious, I can use trapped flies as sentries. Flies will live a long time trapped on tape against a window, and I can monitor everything that goes on without suspicion. And my trained cockroaches can enter rooms, circle the perimeter walls, and then return to me. This will allow me to search out suspect basements. But how do I find which ones to search? It still leaves the problem of where to begin.

Do I need to eat bugs from every neighborhood until I see something? It won't be easy. Or tasty. I'd need water and a flyswatter or net. But if bug memories aren't long, then I can assume the fly I swallowed can't have flown much more than a mile, maybe less. That means the dogs are likely trapped somewhere nearby. Right in my neighborhood.

Every darkened window suddenly seems more menacing. Every person walking past could be a criminal.

"Hey, Bug-boy." I whirl; it's Dog-girl from school. But Dog-girl isn't her real name. What is her name anyway? She's holding back four dogs on their leashes while a fuzzy golden retriever puppy tangles its leash in the legs of the others. One dog swerves onto a lawn and takes a dump. She frowns at me.

"It's not a glamorous job," she says as she picks up the dog's mess.

I laugh a little, and my cheeks heat as if I'm somewhere I shouldn't be.

"What are you doing?" she asks.

I swallow and say, "I—I hear there might be a puppy mill in the neighborhood, and I'm thinking about where that could be."

She lifts an eyebrow and says, "Sit!"

I'm already sitting, and I look at the curb.

"The dogs, I mean, not you." The dogs, who are all sitting now, stare at her as if she's a movie star, all except the puppy, who starts barking at a caterpillar inching toward it. The spatters of rain have completely darkened the concrete sidewalk. "A puppy mill, huh? Who says?"

"I—from gossip, you know?" What am I thinking? I can't trust her. I've probably already said too much.

She shrugs. "I guess they'd need lots of dog food. You could ask at the local pet store who's buying. I haven't seen anything."

Rain starts in earnest.

"Whose puppy is that?" I ask as the little fur ball flips onto its back. "Do you know where they got it?"

Dog-girl straightens and begins pulling the dogs away. "You can't go around accusing people of buying from puppy mills."

"Can I talk to the owners?"

"No. Don't hassle my clients," she replies, tugging on the leashes and continuing down the road, water dripping from the tips of her braids.

"Sorry . . ." I shrug and bike home.

I eat dinner in silence while my mom talks about her legal case and my father discusses how I helped sell the car after watching the body language of the couple. I excuse myself to do homework. Once safely in my room with the door taped, I start training the cockroaches. The roachies will only remember the training for a couple of days, but I hope to find the dogs even sooner.

"Okay, Roachies," I say. "Are you ready for a workout?"

They hiss in reply. Good enough for me. I try not to think of the fact that I'm training them so I can eat them. Maybe I'll get lucky and have a hit at the pet store and I won't have to eat any bugs.

"Who wants to go first?"

Even though Bent seems to be straining to be picked, I choose a different roachie. To start, I set it free on my bedroom floor, snap my fingers, and watch what happens. Roachie scurries about, but in no particular direction. Next, I place it at the door and set sugar cubes in each corner of the room. The path to each cube is clear, but roachies can climb well anyway. Cockroaches also have keen senses of smell. When I snap my fingers, Roachie trots to the first cube, but doesn't bother going to any of the others, and why would it? It has all the food it can handle with one.

After some more trial and error, I leave a single grain of sugar in each corner. This time, after I snap, it travels to the first and then on to the second. I smile. An hour later, I have it marching about the perimeter of the room. This might work. Given enough effort, I will have my spies. Not spies . . . sidekicks. Bugs should be Bug-boy's sidekicks, of course. I don't recall any other superhero having edible sidekicks, but there's a first time for everything.

For my sentry fly-cams, all I need to do is bring some clear tape or my bug net to the fly factory that is the family compost bin. Flies circle it, and I'll have no problem collecting them.

Outside, beyond my home, buzz all manner of troops. I am building an army of sidekicks. I'll save the dogs in no time.

Something I haven't felt for a while rushes through me. It's warm. It lightens me. I think it might be hope. Hope for the dogs. Hope that all my passion for bugs is okay. Hope for me. That maybe *this* is my thing.

Chapter 12
Where Jarrod Settles a Case

I've never been to my mom's office. I've always imagined her in a cubicle somewhere arguing with people on the phone. We walk off an elevator, the doors a burnished silver, and step directly into the lavish legal offices of Cartsen, Collson, Vendetta, and Narrs; the name is written in gold letters over a massive reception desk.

A woman with a headset lifts her head, stares at my helmet, and after seeing my mother, smiles and looks back down at her screen, talking into a microphone. A youngish man with wavy dark hair, who must have been waiting in ambush, approaches from our right flank. He's wearing a neat black suit and a worried look on his face.

"It's off the table," he hisses. Three other suits lounge in high leather-backed chairs in the waiting area, sipping cappuccinos and staring at phones.

My mom takes the wavy-haired man by the elbow and walks him out of the atrium and into the hallway. I hustle along with them.

"The settlement?" she whispers. "Please tell me you're not saying they're refusing the settlement." I'm almost between the two, and she stares at me with an expression that says she regrets bringing me along. Her fingers are spinning her rings again. "Jarrod, this is my assistant, Assaf."

I shake Assaf's hand, but then they're back to business.

"They want a lower amount," Assaf says. "Half."

"Half—but they'd agreed!" My mom glances left and right and then lowers her voice. "They agreed."

"Not anymore. They're here in the Pine boardroom," Assaf says.

This isn't good. My mom expected today to be about finalizing details, not negotiating the biggest deal of her career.

She presses her lips together. "Here's what we're going to do. Move them to the Oak boardroom; it's more imposing. Then gather the team."

Assaf nods and then struts down the hall.

My mom looks at me and huffs. "You have stuff to do?" I pat my backpack, which contains video games, a couple of books, and an apple. "Good, I'll put you in Pine after they're out of it." She grips my shoulder and steers me toward the boardroom. Naming the boardrooms after different trees seems like a desperate attempt to make the legal firm seem greener. I've seen the reams of paper my mom generates and the reams more that she shreds. Trust me, it's not an environmentally friendly business.

We wait at Pine's door as Assaf escorts a bunch of people down the hall. The room where my mom wants to store me for the day has a massive table—I assume it's made of pine, but who knows? Dozens of black leather chairs with high backs ring it. Dirty coffee cups are strewn about one corner, and someone has left a blank legal pad and pen. I wonder just how the Oak boardroom manages to be any more intimidating. This one is the sort of place where I imagine villains plot to take over the world.

I sit at the clean end of the table and unzip my backpack, pulling out my game system and books. As I power up, a man enters wearing a pink shirt and a big, sly grin. I narrow my eyes at him. Without saying a word, he collects the pen and legal pad. Before he leaves, presumably off to do battle with my mother, he slaps the legal pad down on the table and kills a fly. I don't like him at all.

Later, I hear shouting, but I'm busy collecting new weapons and health on my game. I do glance up whenever my mom yells, though. Even though it's muffled, I can tell when it's her. She only shouts when she's really frustrated, so this must be bad. I'm sorry that her case isn't going well, but there's nothing I can do. Even Bug-boy's powers have their limits.

Half an hour passes, and then the handle turns on the door. My mom says nothing, just enters carrying a stack of legal documents that she thuds onto the tabletop. She buries her face in her hands when she sits down. I play for another minute, but she doesn't move. The paper stack teeters. Finally, I put the game down.

"You okay, Mom?" I ask.

I listen to her breathe through her fingers. I've never seen her quite so upset and assume it's the case crumbling that's causing it.

"Maybe I can help?" I ask. "Like I did with Dad? Eat a bug for you after they've had a chance to talk or something?"

At first, she doesn't do anything. Then her hands begin to shake. She rubs them up and down over her face.

"Eat a bug," she says, removing her hands. And then bursts out laughing, but not in a jolly way, more like a mad-scientist-about-to-switch-on-the-electricity type of laughter. "Yes, Jarrod, maybe you can eat a bug and help me. That makes a great deal of sense. I'll just take the information from a fly and use it in my settlement negotiations. I'll make partner for sure." She giggles until she starts to shake her head and then stares at knots in the wood tabletop, silent and unmoving.

I know when I'm being made fun of, but maybe this is my chance to prove to her that I'm not insane. The people she's fighting against worked in here too and it's possible they said something she can use. But how can I learn it if none of the bugs in here would have a useful memory? Perhaps she'll believe me if she sees how eating bugs causes the moment? I inspect the room for insects. I peer into the corners of the ceiling and spot a fat spider—no thanks. A fly bounces against a window.

"Sorry, it's for a good cause," I say. And I slap it with my hand so that it drops to the sill. I sit down on the floor and pop the bug in my mouth.

"Watch this, Mom," I say and then swallow.

I spend most of the next minute bonking my head off glass, staring down a dozen stories to the busy road. I can see boats on the canal and hear a muffled discussion behind me, but none of the words. Then the fly turns, and I see my mom and me. Then I watch myself stand and drive the fly into the glass like it's a windshield

I'm back on the floor.

"Don't do this to yourself," my mom says, near tears and kneeling at my shoulder. "You're causing the moments—*you* are!"

"Gavin believes me, Mom, and you know how smart he is. I know it works."

But there's nothing I saw or heard that I can use to convince her.

"I'm spending too much time at work, I'm sorry. I've lost sight of what's important," she's saying. "We need more tests. Specialists."

Then I remember the fly the man killed. That one might still have a memory!

"Wait," I say and push up off the floor.

"What are you doing, Jarrod? What's happening?" She climbs to her feet as I stumble to the far end of the table.

"I need to find the dead fly," I say.

"Jarrod," she shouts, and the tone is one that demands attention. But the fly lies on the tabletop, and I flick it into my palm. "Jarrod! I forbid you."

I swallow the fly.

Three women and six men. One of them speaks to the others in a language that sounds like German. Then they switch to English when Assaf pokes his head through the door and asks them to follow him.

"Jarrod, Jarrod." My mom's shaking me. "Stop this. Stop it."

I'm lying on the ground again. My nose is sore from where I must have squashed it against the table. Seeing me conscious, my mom sags. "I have to go, honey, are you all right?"

"I got it this time," I say. "Nine, Mom, nine people. Three

women and six men. One speaks German or something like that. I couldn't understand what they were saying."

My mom cocks her head to one side. "You saw them as they left the boardroom this morning. You could have counted them then."

"No—" I say. "Well, yes, but not all of them, and I wasn't paying attention then."

"You could hear them speaking while in here," she adds. "Through the wall. You probably heard the German accent."

"I couldn't hear much," I say. "Maybe a little shouting." I'm not convincing her.

"We'll talk about this later, Jarrod; you are having a lot more moments lately. I've never seen you have two in a row like that. Not since strawberry picking. We'll go see the doctor to determine if anything has changed."

"No, Mom, I can help you. How can I prove it to you?" She's already walking away, striding toward the door. Her shoulders have slouched—she's going to cave. I shut my eyes and try to remember. "One man has a gold tie clip. Another these diamond cuff links. Two have no ties, one a pink shirt. There's a clicking sound, maybe someone tapping a fingernail. The fly wasn't facing them for long enough, so I don't know." My mom's footsteps have halted.

"It's a pen, the clicking sound," she says. "The man in the pink shirt clicks it incessantly . . . You really got all that from eating a fly?" she asks in a flat, even tone.

I nod. "Really."

"This makes no sense. It's impossible." She walks back to me, hands on her hips, and towers over me. "What is in the hair of the women?"

I think back. And it's cool, because I actually remember a lot. "The blonde has something like chopsticks. The brunette, nothing." My mom grimaces. "I helped Dad sell a car, Mom. I knew what you'd said about the report cards—Dad didn't tell me. A bug did."

My mom kneels and holds her chin between her thumb and forefinger. She's thinking. "They're discussing what they're prepared to do right now . . ." she says with a crazy little laugh. "No, no, this is nonsense. I need to work."

"Mom, what did I get on my report card?" She squints. "Do you really think I would have remembered all that from this morning, seeing them walk past? I am not that smart." What does she have to lose?

"No, no, I don't think anyone would have," she replies with a faraway look.

"Are these good people, Mom?"

"What they're trying to do isn't good."

"Then let me help."

Air whistles out of her nose as she sighs. "Okay, Jarrod, let's see what you can do." Her pantsuit snaps as she walks to the door. I hear the neighboring door open and a muffled apology.

I don't know what's she's doing, but I feel better. A minute later she returns with a spider, its legs balled up to its abdomen. My mom slides it in front of me on a sheet of paper.

"Sorry," my mom says. "It's all I could find." I can tell how desperate she is, that this is pretty much the lowest she's ever stooped in her lifetime, asking me to swallow a bug for her.

I've never eaten a spider—not that I know of. Technically

they're not bugs. This one's abdomen is swollen with eggs. But I want her to believe. I need her to.

"I think I'm going to need a glass of water," I say. "And a bucket—just in case."

Chapter 13
Where Jarrod Tries Something Big

"Spiders are not insects," I say.

My mom has placed a glass of water in front of me. A garbage can is at my side.

"Will it work?" she asks. "We only have a few more minutes, and I need to brief my team."

"It might." *If I can keep it down.*

"I don't have time to find a new bug." She slaps her forehead. "What am I saying? You can't do this. This isn't possible. Don't—"

But I am. I draw a deep breath. My mom holds hers. I pick up the sheet of paper, curve it to create a kind of funnel, and shake the spider into my mouth. It lands on my tongue. The expression on my mother's face is of such horror that I'd laugh if I didn't feel so much like vomiting. Holding my head still, I reach for both the garbage can and the glass of water. I chug the water down and flip backward.

"She's gone," the woman with chopsticks in her hair says. She also sports a pencil-eraser-like mole on her cheek. Everyone is upside down.

I'm the spider. I can even see fangs as I advance on a fly twitching in a web. Each time the fly flaps its wings it grows more entangled in spider silk. The people are below me in a room lined with bookshelves packed with huge tomes. Every inch of the walls is covered in dark wood or ancient books that look like something wizards might need for spell casting.

"Well, you were right," pink shirt dude replies, clicking his pen. "They are willing to take less. I don't think they even know about article seventeen of the settlement; they missed it entirely."

I'm near the fly now, and I really don't want to be party to what the spider does next.

The man with the diamond cuff links leans forward. "Finish this. I don't want this going to trial. Fifty million, a hundred million, or two hundred million. The agreed-upon settlement is already less than we'd expected. We've won. This back and forth is taking unnecessary risks."

"But they don't know that," Pen Clicker replies. "My job is to get you the best possible deal."

I rear up and grip the fly with my legs, looping more and more silk around it. The fly buzzes as it seeks to escape, muffling some of what's going on below.

"They don't know that," Cuff Links agrees. "I am only worried this can backfire if we string it out."

"So, what's the final number?" asks the woman with the chopsticks.

"Thirty," Pen Clicker says as he glances around the table at everyone. Each nods in turn.

Finally, the fangs sink into the fly, and I imagine venom coursing into it.

"Sorry," my mom says after a brief knock. "Just something that's been bothering me. The cleaners are terrified of bugs, and I need to get this one before it escapes." Everyone watches with raised eyebrows as my mom tries to snatch the spider from the ceiling and misses. The world streaks as I tumble to the table. Then I'm scurrying toward Chopsticks Woman, who screams. Pen Clicker looms and smacks me with his legal pad.

And I'm back with my mom.

My mom's looking at me with a feverish sheen in her eyes.

"Well?" she asks.

"Thirty," I say. "They're coming back with thirty."

Her fingers tighten into a fist that she holds at her shoulder. "Pretty good," she says. "Not terrible. Wait—you *actually* heard this?"

I nod and continue. "But the guy with diamond cuff links really doesn't want to go to trial. He said fifty, one hundred, two hundred million—no trial."

My mom's eyes widen. "They don't want a trial. Anything else?"

"Something about missing article seventeen."

"Article seventeen, how would you know anything about articles?" She frowns and jogs around the table to her stack of documents.

Assaf knocks and thrusts his head around the door. "You ready?"

She shows him the palm of her hand to get him to wait as she flips through the legal documents. "Who added article seventeen?" she asks, and then she makes a choking sound as she reads "No, no, no." Without further discussion, she marches out of the room and back into the Oak boardroom.

I run to the wall and press my ear against it. I really wish I could be a fly on the wall now.

The documents slap onto their table, and my mom shouts, "Trial!" And then the door shuts. After a few minutes, I give up trying to hear and pick up my video game.

Two hours later, my mom walks back into the Pine boardroom and grins. Then she comes and picks me up in a hug like I'm five years old.

"Mom, Mom, stop," I say. "I almost have a new high score."

"Oh, Jarrod, but we do have a new high score. We did it!" she says and gives me another squeeze before setting me back down. My screen reads *Game Over*.

For some reason I can't get excited by my mom's announcement. But she doesn't seem to notice.

"Do you know how much we settled for?" she asks, beaming. "Guess, just guess. Go ahead."

I shrug. "Thirty million?"

"No," she says and smacks me on the shoulder. "Higher."

"Fifty," I say. It all sounds like an awful lot of money.

"One hundred and ten million dollars," she says, sounding out every syllable to make it even bigger.

"Wow, an eighty-million-dollar spider," I say and flash a smile that I don't feel. Why am I not happy for her?

A woman in a navy dress that I think my mom has in her closet too comes in and says, "Arlene, I just heard. Congratulations."

"Oh!" My mom smooths out her jacket. "Jennifer, please let me introduce you to my son, Jarrod. Jarrod, this is Ms. Narrs."

"I recognize your name," I say.

She nods. "Would you like to see your mom's name up on the company letterhead one day?"

I actually don't really care, but I know that's what my mom wants, so I smile. Narrs winks back at my mom, who flushes and straightens her jacket again.

"We'll talk later," Ms. Narrs says. "Celebrate."

After she leaves, my mom starts twisting one ring after another.

"You can't tell anyone," she whispers to me. "About this bug-eating business. About what happened."

And I swallow. This is why I don't feel happy for her. Isn't it sort of cheating, even if it's for a good reason? I may have found my thing, but maybe I'm not doing it right. Not at all.

Chapter 14
Where Jarrod Gathers His Soldiers

For the rest of the day, my mom does anything I want. Maybe she's feeling guilty about feeding me a spider, or maybe she's just shining from her huge win. Whatever it is, it gets me home early, which is great because I need some time to train the cockroaches and to begin my reconnaissance mission. *Ugh.* More bugs to eat. But there are dogs somewhere out there who aren't allowed to go outside. Who might never have felt the grass beneath their paws. Have never had the joy of catching a Frisbee between their teeth. Who are suffering.

I have another email from Gavin.

Hello? Biggest thing that's ever happened to you and I don't even get an email? Where are you? I'm sending an illicit message during computer science class and—

He must have got caught.

"You want a snack, honey?" my mom asks from the kitchen. "Bowl of ice cream? Order a pizza?"

Any other day I'd say yes, but for now I think I'd better keep my stomach empty.

"No thanks, Mom. I'm going for a bike ride in a bit." She

knows how normal biking helps me feel.

I reply to Gavin. *Sorry, Gav, my mom's been keeping me under her thumb. I have to tell you about something—something really big. I'll catch you after school.*

"Maybe we should get you a mask?" my mom continues. "So you don't swallow a bug while biking."

"Sure, why don't I get a full mask like Darth Vader, and then no one will make fun of me."

"Sorry, honey—" she begins. "I'm still finding this difficult to swallow—ouch—bad pun, sorry again. Do you want to come out to a late lunch with Dad and me? We're celebrating. Everything!"

"No thanks," I call back, and a little later I hear her leave.

I hit send on my email. A walking stick crawls across the top of the computer monitor. Is there any way I can avoid my plan? Maybe—

"Okay, Twig," I say to the walking stick. "Let's try one more option before resorting to bug-murder—insecticide."

Before I start my killing spree, I bring up Google Maps and use Google Street View to search the neighborhood in the hope of narrowing my search. I know for a fact that the driveway wasn't cobblestone, but that only eliminates one in ten prospective homes. A tenth of what's left have no driveways at all. And of the remaining eighty percent, there are a few apartment buildings. But that still leaves me a whole lot of houses and the same search area. No, I do need my bug-cams. It's time.

I push out the front door. Once on my bike, I pedal first to the pet store, where they tell me that they'll keep an eye out for large orders, but don't really help. I don't really like being in the store. The only bugs they have are those they keep to feed to their reptiles. I ride back into the neighborhood for a block before slowing to a stop. What am I looking for?

I need to find bugs or spiders with a good view of an area. I'll squish them, mark off their address, and eat them back at home. One bug per five houses, per street, for a mile in every direction of where I first swallowed the fly. In my backpack I have brought my creative writing journal. It's supposed to be for keeping a diary, but it'll work well for what I have in mind. In its pages I sketch a map of the streets. I don't remember all their names, but the pattern's easy. Just a grid without many curvy roads. It's nearing three o'clock, so I don't have much time—I'll have to swing by Gavin's for help once school's out.

First, I bike to where it all started. To where I swallowed the fly—bug-zero. I bend to pick up a tiny beetle, but then realize a beetle isn't a good choice. A beetle's more interested in what's on the ground, or worse, under the ground. It might be cool to check out what it's like to live as a beetle, but not now. For now, I need something that will have a good view. And, since I'm planning to eat so many bugs, maybe a bug that doesn't fly is a better choice. A caterpillar slips down on a thread again.

People eat caterpillars, I tell myself. But I don't think they see very well, but then flies don't see very far, and that doesn't seem to matter. My bug memories aren't all faceted like a fly's vision. I've never had a moment in the ultraviolet or infrared light spectrums either, and that's how other bugs like bees and mosquitoes see. No, my brain seems to translate whatever the bugs see into something I can understand. Hadn't Gavin started saying something about that? Now that I think of it, Mr. Chang had too; he'd said our brains are amazingly similar to insects'. But I don't really need to know how it works, only that it does.

I catch the caterpillar in cupped hands. It rears up with the fuzzy little body coming half off my palm, legs scrabbling.

I have to test my theory. Better that then to collect dozens of caterpillars and then have nothing. It would be irresponsible to kill bugs without a reason. How many bugs equal the life of a dog? With a sigh, I lie down on the same grass near where I fell. I don't even squish the caterpillar. I don't want to see what's inside. I intend to swallow it whole. With a water bottle, I chase the bug down my throat. The fuzz gets caught for a second, but another gulp pushes it the rest of the way.

And there I go.

Perched on a leaf, nibbling away, I'm very pleased that I don't have the caterpillar's sense of taste. What amazes me is the incredible energy I draw from being so close to the leaf, as if I'm saturated by its oxygen. People walk by as the caterpillar mows down. I spot a man in a cowboy hat. A woman pushing a stroller. What am I hoping to see? A clue. Something suspicious. A car races down the street. A white van. This memory's longer than I expect. Caterpillar-cams are going to be perfect. I study more cars and passersby, some with dogs; one dog is even a golden retriever like the puppies. But no one seems like the kind of person who would abuse animals. But then, who would?

Just before I wake, a construction truck motors down the road. Something about it makes me track it, but I haven't decided why a construction truck would be a clue. But what I do know is that caterpillars work. And they're a very good choice if you need to eat lots of bugs. Why? Because caterpillars can be fried.

Then I'm sailing down on a thread of silk without any thought to the doom to which I drop.

I wake to kids walking past me on their way home from school. They step over my legs and look at me as if I might be a little bit dangerous.

I bike over to Gavin's house, catching him as he steps onto his driveway.

"So, what's the big news?" he asks.

"I'm so glad you're here," I say. "You need to help me collect caterpillars."

"Why? What's going on? I got your email. What's big?"

So, I explain. I tell him about helping sell a car for my dad. I even tell him about how I helped my mom with her case. And then I tell him about the dogs in their cages and my call with the police.

"You actually told the police that you ate a fly and saw what it saw?" Gavin asks.

We're both silent for a few seconds before Gavin bursts into laughter. Then I start to laugh too.

"Hello, police," Gavin imitates me. "Yes, I just witnessed a murder. Although technically I didn't witness it. A bumblebee I ate did. Can you help?"

He's laughing a little harder than me now. Still, it is funny.

"So how are you going to find the dogs?" he asks, his voice growing serious again.

I tell him my plan to harvest caterpillar-cams.

"That could work," he agrees, "but you'd have to get lucky."

He doesn't talk about more experiments to determine if my superpower is real.

"What about trying to buy a puppy?" he asks. "Wouldn't they be selling the puppies?"

See, he's smart.

"Good idea! And no bugs necessary," I say. "But these dogs don't have time for trial and error. We have to do *everything*."

"Tell you what," he says, "I'll help collect for an hour, but then I'll go online and see if I can buy a puppy from someone in the city."

We high-five.

With the plan in place, we check my street grid and bike to the far corner of it. He'll take one side of the street, and I'll take the other. This will ensure that I'm getting a good overview. Before we start, I point out the types of caterpillars I want. The only caterpillars I ask him to leave alone are the ones that turn into monarch butterflies. They're endangered, and I know for a fact that they're poisonous because of the milkweed they eat. But it's not the right time of year for them anyway, and I can count the number of monarchs I found this summer on my fingers, so I'm not too worried about Gavin bringing me any.

I pick the first caterpillar from the low-hanging branch of a birch tree that stretches over the sidewalk. The caterpillar is small and green, but most of them are fuzzy orange and black ones: Pyrrharctia isabella. It's a fall caterpillar. Most species have already turned into moths or butterflies, but these guys freeze solid during winter and then thaw with spring.

I place the green caterpillar in between the first two pages of the book and then slam it closed. When I open it, goo sticks to both pages. The caterpillar is dead.

"Thank you for your sacrifice, little buddy," I say, and then take two Gavin has collected from across the street. I bike ten doors down to search out the next victim. I'm glad to have Gavin's help, as I'd never have been able to collect enough on my own. We scramble up tree trunks. We sneak into garden bushes.

"What are you doing?" an old lady asks. She's using an umbrella, even though it's not raining.

"Bug collecting," I reply, and it's totally true. I sense her eyes on me as I continue, but she's the only one who asks. Most people walk right by without a second glance, in a hurry to get somewhere or texting and not even looking up. The rush-hour parents stroller their kids home from daycare, and a number of them give me strange looks, but no one stops me.

In a few places I settle for the fuzzy yellow and green caterpillars I keep seeing flattened on the road. I write down the address for each bug, and then place the caterpillar in the page of the book before slamming it closed.

"This must suck for you," Gavin says as I crush another of his.

I nod. It does sadden me that all these caterpillars aren't going to become butterflies or moths, but then I think of the dogs in the basement, which if I do nothing, won't live. They'll never have a chance to feel the sun on their fur or leap into cool water on a hot day.

"Okay, that's about all the bug picking I can handle," Gavin says. "I promised my mom I'd be home in an hour—I'll let you know about buying a puppy!"

I thank him and watch him ride off.

An hour later, the sun slips below rooftops. Dusk has settled on the neighborhood by the time I slam the pages of the book closed for the final time. A couple streets remain, but I've collected on all the others. I've also filled the last page in my book. It's swollen with caterpillar goo, and I hold it in my hand as I bike for fear of the goo covering my knapsack.

There are two hundred pages in my book, with one caterpillar between every two pages. A hundred caterpillars to eat.

Barf-o-rama. But I don't need to worry about that now. Tomorrow. Tomorrow, I'll feign sick and eat my army.

Chapter 15
Where Jarrod Eats His Army

My breakfast is two eggs, hard-boiled and unpeeled. I also have a box of Fruit Loops, one of those single-serving sizes you sometimes get at hotels or for camping, and a small carton of unopened milk. My mom's going a bit crazy trying to keep bugs out of my diet.

Last night, she racked her brain for something guaranteed to be bug-free and settled on cooked peas, Jell-O, meat—still in the package—and a peeled potato. She strained the water out of the tap and peeled the potato at the table.

"This is huge," my dad says as he takes a bite of his scrambled eggs.

"Do you—" I'm hesitant because I don't really want him to say yes. "Do you want me to show you? Prove it? You know? Eat a bug for you?"

"I believe," my dad says. "I've got a fatter commission check coming this month because of your help."

"I have an idea." My mom has her finger in the air like it's some eureka moment. "Why doesn't your father keep a fly near the water cooler. He can bring it home whenever he needs some help? Flies work, don't they, Jarrod?"

I swallow a little of my breakfast cereal. "I don't feel so good," I say. I had a nightmare about waking to find my praying mantis eating my head. Revenge for her buddies.

"All this talk of eating bugs, I don't blame you, son," my dad replies.

"I'm just glad we know what's causing your moments. This could be far worse," my mom adds.

"Worse? This is great," my dad says. "My son's a superhero. Wait a second . . ." My dad shoots out of his chair and swats a fly on the kitchen counter.

"No, Dad!" I say. "I really don't want to eat bugs if I don't have to."

But my dad's not listening. With the wings between his fingers, he drops it in his mouth.

"Coffee, coffee," he moans. Then looks madly for his cup before using the tap at the sink. He swallows and stands looking at us with his arms out for balance.

"What?" he says. "It could be genetic."

I roll my eyes. "This isn't making me feel better."

"Go lie down," my mom says. She cups her cool palm on my forehead. "If you feel better, you can go to school after lunch. Do you want me to stay home with you?"

"No way," I blurt, and then say softer, "No, sorry. I know you have to do your . . . stuff. I'm not a baby. I'll be okay."

"I'll call the school," she says.

I emailed Gavin that I'm planning to pretend to be sick. I hope he can blow off school too, but that's asking a lot of a guy like Gavin. After all, school is his thing.

I stand, and my dad slaps me on the back. "Even Superman needs to take breaks," he says.

Funny, but acting sick makes me feel a little sick. I trudge to my bedroom, pull the tape off my door and enter the room. Staring at all my bugs, I feel ashamed. I am using them. Murdering them by the dozen. Eating them to save dogs—is it a fair trade? Dog-girl would say so. And after thinking about the dog's festering wound, or the one blinded by an eye infection, I know I'm doing the right thing.

"Sorry, buddies," I say. "It's an emergency." I fail to add that the damage is already done.

My book of caterpillars is on my desk. I can't imagine the horror my bugs would feel if they knew it was caterpillar blood seeping through the pages.

I feel a little more ill, but it's not the flu or anything. I'm anticipating my day.

There's a knock at my door. "We're off, honey," my mom says, but she doesn't open the door. "You sure you're okay?"

"Yes, Mom! Have a good day," I shout back.

Soon my parents depart for work, leaving me home alone. I email Gavin. *You there?* But there's no reply.

I double-check to ensure my parents have left and then shut and tape my bedroom door. No bug should have to witness what happens next. Seeing no reason to delay, I fire up a pan of oil and then open my journal. I have to pull the first two pages apart. With the flat of a knife, I scrape the first caterpillar off and drop it into the pan. It sizzles and pops. The fuzz disappears and I breathe a sigh of relief. While the caterpillar cooks, I lay out sheets of clean paper and rewrite the addresses. Once the caterpillar has gone crispy and brown, I place it on the address where I found it. I lay them out in the pattern of the map.

Each bug takes a couple of minutes to fry, but I can keep track of six without getting them mixed up in the pan. Even so, an hour goes by before I shut off the gas to the stove. Oil has spattered all over the counters and backsplash. Legs and antennae dot the pan. The map looks like some weird bug buffet, and I shudder. What's worse, though, is that it all smells pretty darn good, and it's around snack time. My stomach rumbles.

"Traitor," I say.

I decide to start with the address closest to where I swallowed the fly and work my way outward in a ring. I salt and pepper the first of my insect feast, and then there's nothing to be done except eat.

As I hold the first caterpillar between my fingers, all I can think is how crispy the formerly black and orange, rather squishy bug now seems. I put it in my mouth and am about to swallow it with the help of some water when I realize . . . it's actually quite tasty. I don't need any water. I crunch down, and hot goo fills my mouth. Nutty. Peppery. Is that maple flavor? I swallow, choking a little on an extra crispy bit.

And then I'm in a tree, and I can see that it is, in fact, the red leaves of a maple tree that I'm chewing. But the leaf is blocking my view, and I have to wait until the caterpillar eats a hole through it before I can see the sidewalk through a dappling of other leaves. I listen for sounds, creaks, bells, laughter of kids. Nothing. I sniff deeply, but all I take in is the rich, oxygenated air of the tree—no tar smell.

Not one person walks by before I'm back in the kitchen. The

clock tells me five minutes have gone by. On the positive side, I didn't see a single maggot or dog dropping. Ignoring my glass of water, I salt and then eat the next caterpillar, which must have been one the green ones because the gunk inside slimes over my tongue. I struggle to my feet, nearly heaving before I reach the water. I chug it back. The glass shatters on the floor as I drop.

It's almost dark. I'm on a tree trunk inching downward, my legs slipping easily over rough bark. Below me, a couple argues about whether to let a set of aging parents come and stay with them. It's a private conversation, and I feel bad because I can't shut it out. The voices rise and fall as if they keep forgetting themselves until the man strides off and leaves the woman in tears. "I've had enough," she says to herself. To the caterpillar. And then I'm on the kitchen floor in a puddle of water and glass.

I take a break. Glass tinkles as I sweep it into a pile and then mop the water. I already feel as though I've run a marathon. But I have to keep going. If I stop, I'll never start again. I find a plastic glass in a cabinet and fill it with water.

I get the curry powder and spice up the next few. Several caterpillars later with nothing but leaf eating and the sounds of traffic, I eat another bad one. Remember the fuzzy yellow and green ones? Yeah, don't eat them. It's not the hair. It's what's inside. Even grosser than the green ones. I get it near the back of my tongue and then start to gag and vomit into the sink. I don't even have a moment.

I'm onto a new street and start off easy with a crispy black and orange bug.

In this scene, I can survey the road, and I smell the burnt rubber before I see the source. I squint as a city construction pickup rattles past, dragging a trailer heaped with hot asphalt.

Construction! That's it! It's why I wondered after the construction truck I'd seen. That's one of my only real clues. The smell of tar. Someone was paving a driveway or the road nearby. If I can find the local areas of construction, I can narrow down the houses to within smelling range. I munch through the rest of the caterpillars and mark down anything that appears construction related. The only two caterpillars I leave behind are fuzzy yellow-green ones.

After all the bug eating, I look at my notebook. I've noted four locations where construction was ongoing or recently completed. And in the backyard of one house, I saw a fenced-in area that could be used for exercising dogs. I note the location of everything. After six hours of superhero bug eating, it's time to enter phase two.

Chapter 16
Where Jarrod Takes Off His Helmet

First, I take the roachies on another training run. This time, I sneak them out of my room to our basement to practice on foreign terrain. There are more basements to survey than I can handle with my four cockroaches, but I want my elite troops trained and ready for when I need them. All but Bent perform well. By the time I'm done, it's almost four o'clock.

There's a knock at the door, and there stands Gavin, sweat coursing down his face. "Sorry I bailed," he says. "I tried, but I was actually feeling sicker about not going to school than actually pretending to be sick. My mom even asked if I should stay home, and I said, 'No! I have to go!' She almost made me stay home. I would've barfed for sure."

"It's okay, Gav, you're here now. Today got pretty crazy for me."

"Did you do it? Eat the caterpillars?" he asks.

I show him into the kitchen, and he stays at the door. Bug bits are everywhere.

"It's a bug slaughterhouse," he whispers. "An abbugatoir."

I don't feel good about it, but I force a smile. "Fry them for two minutes, salt, a touch of pepper, and a drop of lemon juice."

"You're the man," he says. "I've had three hits for puppies, but no one from the area. Though, if I ran a puppy mill, I wouldn't sell the puppies in the same city, so I think we'd have to buy a few puppies and then tail the seller, and since neither of us can drive . . . Well, what did you learn from . . .?" His hand sweeps the carnage.

I explain to him the road repair smell clue and the dog clue, and he agrees that the smell clue is the better bet, because it didn't look like the dogs were getting out during my moment.

"Let's decide if any of the construction areas make sense, then bug the nearby houses that match what we know," Gavin says. "Wait—what do we know?"

"Only that the driveway's paved and the house has a basement."

"Okay—let's go," he says.

First, we head to the fly factory to collect the rest of the troops. Our compost bin is on the back porch. When it's hot like it is now, the larvae go from egg to fly in the matter of a day. Hundreds of maggots inch along the green bin's surface, but I'm interested only in the flies buzzing around it.

"Foul and repugnant," Gavin says and covers his mouth.

"And what do you think happens to your body after you're dead?" I ask. "You're a bug-nursery playground."

"If I die today, tell my parents to cremate me."

With a butterfly net that I use for catching insects, I snare one fly after another and place them in small jam jars.

"What are you doing with the flies?" Gavin asks, his hand muffled by his fingers.

"I'm going to stick them to windows using clear packing tape. That way I'll be sure to know which way they're facing."

"Fly-cams, awesome," he replies, and the amazement in his eyes is genuine. I realize it's been a while since I've seen that look on his face. On anyone's face.

The jars clink as I place them in my backpack. Then we head out on our bikes. I still feel a little queasy from the hundred or so bugs I had for lunch. The hot sun beats down as we weave around joggers and parents pushing strollers. Traffic is light. On the way, I tell Gavin everything I can remember from my moment with the dogs. What I saw, heard, and smelled. At the first location—identified by a former caterpillar spy as a construction site—we search for houses that have basements and paved driveways. On either side of a road, sporting a recently repaired dark patch of pavement, there are over a dozen houses that match the description.

"There could be more. That tar smell can travel pretty far," Gavin says.

"Well, we can't eliminate this area, but let's see what the others look like."

He agrees, and we pedal until the lights of a construction truck flash orange at a corner.

"It's the smell," I say and swallow. "I remember this caterpillar. I'd caught the whiff of tar then, but construction hadn't been ongoing, so it wasn't this powerful."

Gavin points to a large two-story house with a basement window well.

"Let's bike closer," I say. The sounds of a jackhammer thunder in my ears, so it's impossible to listen for creaks or bells.

Smoke trails off the road surface as a paver rolls over it, smoothing and compacting fresh blacktop. As with the first location, there are over two dozen prospective homes. I shake my head.

"I don't think this is it," I shout over the noise.

"Why not?" Gavin says. "We have tar."

"Let's keep looking." I bike on.

Beside me, Gavin counts until he reaches ten.

"I can smell the tar for half a block, ten houses," he explains.

It's the quiet I notice most about this next spot. A park stretches along one side of the road. The only reminder that construction occurred here is the ribbons of black used to fill cracks in the pavement.

We head for the park, and I lean my bike against the playground slide. Gavin lowers his kickstand.

"If it's either of the other two spots, we're looking at forty homes on either side, more if we consider other streets."

He sits on a swing and begins to throw his legs backward and forward to get it going.

Creak, creak. Creak, creak.

And then I know.

"Gavin!" I say and lower my voice, reminding myself of what kind of person must live nearby. "This is it. The creaking sound, it was the swing. It was from the park."

It's as though a chill has settled about our shoulders and the neighborhood.

Gavin shudders and glances around furtively. "Let's finish this then."

We count ten homes from the tar and eliminate those

without basements or with cobblestone driveways.

With Gavin keeping watch—the agreed-upon emergency signal being two owl hoots—I wander up to the front garden of the first and prep a fly by holding the tape over top of the jar and shaking it until the fly's stuck. I cut the tape and press it against the window. Perfect. If I didn't know it was there, I wouldn't see it.

On the way out, I trip over a garden gnome and fall onto the lawn, the jars clinking in my pack.

"You need to be careful," Gavin says, glancing left and right, but no one's around to spot us. "How are you going to explain taping flies to windows?"

I don't have an answer for that. My next target is two doors down, and we walk the distance, pushing our bikes by the seats.

The driveway has an old purple Corvette in it. People speak near the front window, so after I prepare my fly, I slip to the side of the house while Gavin hides behind a tree. The basement windows are dark, so I tape the fly-cam on the kitchen windowpane.

Hoot-hoot! Hoot-hoot!

I freeze and grab my bag to run, but I can already see that it's too late. The driveway ends in a fence. The only escape is the front yard, and Gavin has signaled that people are out. There's nothing to be done but think of a reason for being there.

"Excuse me?" A woman stands on the porch as I jog back down the driveway. She's wearing a lot of denim, some of it patched with angel wings and skulls.

"Oh, sorry," I say, brilliant guy that I am.

"Can I help you?" The way she's asking, I know what she's really saying. *Do I need to call the police?*

"No, I . . . uh." I point to my bike for some reason. I left it on the sidewalk for a quick getaway.

"What are you doing in my driveway?" she asks.

Then the answer hits me. "Cool car," I say. "I love your car. Sixties?"

Her demeanor changes and she says: "1964 Stingray."

I whistle like I'm really impressed. "Wanted a closer look. Sorry to have bugged you."

I walk away and the woman watches me. Gavin emerges from behind the tree and says, "Sorry to have bugged you? Really?"

I shrug. "She caught me off guard."

"We have to find a better excuse," Gavin says, and then runs up onto a porch littered with newspapers. "Here," he says, handing me a community newspaper. "You're now a delivery boy."

But we don't get caught as I plant the remaining ten bugs. By the time we're done, all the homes are pretty much our number-one suspects, but then, that's what the fly-cams were for—narrowing the field even more.

"Jarrod, if your moments are usually within the last minutes of the bug's life, how are you going to learn much?" Gavin asks.

I say: "Bugs sleep, so I think some memories are from before they fall asleep. If we collect in the morning, we'll have some memories from the morning and some the evening and night."

He's giving me that amazed look again.

I really hope this is going to work. I'm frustrated by how long it is taking, but I'm doing my best.

We split up, heading to our respective houses. When I get home, I park my bike on the porch and lock it. After I set my nearly empty knapsack at the door, I pause. What am I doing? I *know* what's causing my moments. Why am I still wearing a stupid helmet? With a nod, I reach up, grab the snap of the helmet, and then yank it off. For almost two years I've borne the stares, the laughter, and the teasing. And now I am free.

A weight lifts from my shoulders. I rake my fingers through my long brown hair. I grab a curl and see that it can reach past my chin if I tug it straight. I scratch at my head and hang my helmet on my handlebars before turning to stroll into the house. Maybe now people will stop treating me like a bug.

I'm not putting my helmet back on ever again.

Chapter 17
Where Jarrod Scares the Teacher

Never is a really long time.

That night my parents and I argue about my wearing the helmet. We made a deal. If I don't have an accidental moment for an entire week, I can take it off in the classroom and at home. I think it's pretty fair. And the negotiation was easier when my dad handed me a fly and asked me to tell him what it knew. Which wasn't very much. He'd kept it alive the whole day and on the way home, so by the time I ate it, all I saw was Dad singing along to the radio. He was pretty good.

The next morning, I peel and eat my eggs for breakfast. Let me tell you, do NOT eat three hardboiled eggs and ninety-seven caterpillars; my mom almost starts crying when I fart. That also means she is happy when I say I'm leaving early to meet Gavin.

I collect the flies I left on windows on the way to school. I'll eat them after school. The only home I am worried about getting caught spying on is the Corvette woman's, but the car is already gone when I arrive. Some of the flies still twitch on their tape as I pull it off the windows and stick it on a scrap of paper with the address. Before filing them away, I end each of their tiny lives. I don't want them remembering anything more. Others are already dead, so I should get a good cross-section of memories.

I'm itching at the edge of a piece of tape when I hear a door open, two doors down.

"Hey!" A man's voice. Deep.

I freeze.

Then comes the sound of ringing. The bell!

"Hey! Come on, kids," yells the man. "Time to get ready for school."

Three kids, sisters I'd guess, climbing on the playground, squeal that they're coming. I tear the tape of the final fly from the window. Hearing the bell is like hearing a death knell. I *know* I have the right area. I want to be away from here.

With the bugs in my bag, I finish my ride and hurry to rack my bike at school.

"Did you get them?" Gavin asks. "The fly-cams?" He's bouncing from foot to foot as I lock up my bike.

I pat my knapsack and start up the stairs into the school.

"And you marked the addresses?" Gavin continues.

"Yes!"

"What about the science test, are you ready for that?" he asks.

I stop.

"Science test? It's the first week of school," I say.

"Oh, I should have told you. Chang announced it at homeroom yesterday. Not that you could have studied really. Oh, man—this afternoon—it's going to be a really hard one." Gavin's eyes widen. "There's only one question on it. It covers everything we learned last year. He'll give a prize if you get one hundred percent."

"It's all right. I suck at tests anyways," I say. I ignore the part about the prize and start climbing. There is no risk of me acing the test.

"Not good, Jarrod. You can't be in gifted science and suck at tests. It's not possible. Chang uses these tests to see who should stay. Besides, you've got your bugs to think about." He frowns. "I should have tried to help you."

I can't tell if he's being serious. "Don't worry about it."

We get to class, and Gavin is not the only one nervous about the test.

"How am I supposed to know what you all studied?" Dog-girl says as I enter the classroom. "I wasn't even here!"

"It's just one question," I say as I slump into my chair. "I'm sure you'll do okay."

Dog-girl swivels her head to me. "Do you think you can help me over lunch break?"

Someone giggles. Everyone here knows my skill level on tests. Everyone except her. She hasn't known me for long enough to realize that I'm a bug to be stepped on. Before I can stop myself, I hear my voice say: "Sure, okay."

Lunch is just prior to the test. That doesn't give me much time to prepare for a review of a year of science. What am I thinking?

"That would be so awesome," she replies. Her dimples are back. I feel like I'm hovering on wings, flimsy fluttery wings that I don't know how to use. Then she opens her binder and faces the teacher as he begins. I'm terrified and clench my desk, knuckles whitening.

Chang waves a sheet of paper, and everyone follows it with

their eyes, knowing what it is. "I've only ever had one student get this question one hundred percent right," he says and lays the paper on his desk. "And she went on to receive her doctorate in organic chemistry." Chang smooths the test and then folds it in half, then in a quarter before slipping the test into his pocket. It's then that I notice the spider crawling across the ceiling. And I have my solution.

"Um, Mr. Chang?"

All eyes pivot to me, and I draw a deep breath.

"Hold . . . completely . . . still," I say, enunciating every syllable.

He freezes.

Everyone knows that I *do* know everything about bugs, so the whole class starts running their hands over their bare arms and mussing up their hair as if something could be in it.

To confirm their suspicions, I reach down and take off my shoe, holding it by the toe.

Mr. Chang takes a step back and starts to move his hand toward the eyeglasses in his shirt pocket.

"No, Mr. Chang, don't do anything!" On the ceiling is a common spider, but he doesn't know that.

"Spider," someone whispers, pointing up.

It's directly above the desk, and Mr. Chang's head tilts back to stare up, but he keeps himself still.

"Black widow," says another student, and I do nothing to discourage the rumor.

Slowly, I walk up to his desk, climb on top, and then whack the spider with the heel of my shoe. It sticks to it.

"Got it," I say, and everyone heaves a sigh of relief. A few even clap.

"Thank you, Jarrod," Chang says, pulling at his shirt collar. "I really don't like spiders. Can those kill?"

"Can a black widow kill?" I echo.

He nods.

"The female's venom is more potent than a rattlesnake's."

"Okay, well thanks again," Chang says with a shudder. "Your bug expertise is appreciated. Back to an only marginally less frightening topic, your field trip approval forms."

I hold the shoe like I'd hold gold. Once back at my desk, I take the tip of my pencil and scrape the spider out of the grooves of the sneaker sole and drop it on the desk.

Gavin turns and winks at me. He knows what I've done.

Dog-girl's eyes are bouncing from the dead spider to my face. She opens her mouth to say something, and I put my finger to my lips and slip my foot back into the shoe. When she isn't watching, I fold the spider into a scrap of paper and slide it into my pocket.

At recess, I find a quiet spot in the yard and eat the spider. It's getting easier killing and eating bugs and spiders. I don't even need water this time. Maybe I'll become something of a bug connoisseur. Is there a job in that? Pairing fine bugs with wine, maybe? I lean back against the tree and swallow. To anyone watching my moment, I will just appear to be sleeping.

I'm staring at Mr. Chang's cowlick of white hair and the paper he's whisking around while he talks about how hard the test is. Then he slaps the paper on the desk, smooths it, and proceeds to fold it. I only have a few seconds to read the question, but it's enough. I know what the test is on.

I jerk forward.

"Gavin!" I call him over. He's got his head in a book, sitting on a boulder. "Come here a minute?"

Gavin shuts his book and wanders over. "Do you know what I think you know?"

I nod. "Do you want to know what you think that I know?"

He pauses, and I sense him wrestling with it. No one knows how I got the question. "We both can't get perfect scores," he says.

I laugh. "Even knowing what I know, I can't get a perfect score. You, on the other hand? You can."

He whistles. "All right. I might not use it, but tell me."

I glance over at a group of girls, Dog-girl among them.

"Okay, but you have to explain to me what it means," I say and write out the test question on a piece of paper. I change all the numbers and wording so that it won't be obvious I saw the question if someone else sees it. When I'm done, Gavin gives a low grunt. "That's really tough. We haven't even done all of this," he says. "Let me work that out."

He sits down beside me and leans against the tree. By the end of recess, he doesn't have the answer, but he's the type of kid that once started can't stop, so he says he'll use part of his computer science class to work through the question on the Internet.

I pass him between classes, and he hands me four pages of proofs. Just in time for lunch.

Chapter 18
Where Jarrod Would Have Aced the Test

"What have you got for lunch?" Dog-girl asks. We're both sitting on the roots of a large oak tree, leaning against the trunk.

I want to ask her name, I really do, but by this time I should know it, so it doesn't seem right.

I crack open my lunch container and sigh at the craziness. "An entire package of baloney, and a can of brown beans." I wave the can opener my mom provided.

Her face sours. "Processed meat causes colon cancer, and brown beans are high in sodium and sugar."

Yes, I want to say, but I balance my diet with bugs. I glance over at what she has.

A small, plain yogurt in a reusable container. Some granola. An apple. And a stainless-steel water bottle.

I'm glad I have a juice box today rather than the usual soda.

"Juice isn't any better for you than soda, you know? Really just sugar and water, unless you squeeze it yourself and leave the pulp."

I hadn't asked. "Thanks."

She shrugs. "Better than bugs, I guess."

And I shake my head furiously. "No, no, bugs are really healthy. Full of protein and fat and iron . . ." I trail off at her look of disgust but then straighten. Maybe it's because I feel like I represent them now, but for whatever reason, I add, "Did you know that if we farmed bugs it would end starvation? And even if we just added bug farming to normal farming, bugs can be farmed on pig and cattle farms by eating their manure, so it's way more environmentally friendly."

As I talk, she starts out with her finger in her mouth pretending to gag, but then slowly takes her hand away and listens.

"It's only weird to eat bugs in places like the United States and Canada," I say. "Lots of people from different cultures eat bugs as a normal part of their diet."

She has a thoughtful look and asks: "Do you? Do you eat bugs?"

I start to say that I do, but instead make a grossed-out face. "What do you think?" I ask and point to my can of beans. "I try to avoid bugs when possible, but did you know that there are bugs in a lot of food already?"

She's staring at me again.

"No, really, regular flour has bugs in it. Pasta is allowed one bug part per gram. And shredded carrots? Eighty bug parts per gram! Canned juices are allowed one maggot per cup and—"

"A maggot, really?"

"Google it!" I grin.

She starts packing away her lunch.

"Sorry, I'll stop," I say.

We sit for a moment, looking at one another. My eyes keep dropping to her bow-shaped lips.

"So . . . the test. We're supposed to be talking about science, right?" And I can't believe I changed the subject to school.

"Right, yeah, science," she says, looking at her yogurt as if it contains bugs. "At my last school we studied some physics, then started on chemistry, but I hadn't gotten very far yet. How far have you gotten?"

I barely know what she's talking about. And I realize that I have nothing to share with her. Nothing except the real question. I look at the proofs Gavin gave me, and it's like reading ancient Egyptian hieroglyphics.

"Gavin and I came up with a question that hits most of the areas we covered last year." I hold the answer sheet out to her. I hadn't meant to do this, I really hadn't, but there it is. At the very least, I should have just given her the question rather than the answer. She wouldn't have time to figure out the solution before the test. "If you can answer something like this, you'll be okay."

She takes the answer, flipping through the pages. "Jarrod," she says after she's done reading it. "Why did you kill that spider?"

She asks a lot of questions. But she hasn't once glanced at my helmet. Everyone always stares at the helmet. She doesn't seem to realize that I'm a bug. She will soon enough. It's then I notice that an ant from the tree has crawled from the tree bark to her shoulder. A shoulder covered in a fuzz of blonde fur. Dog fur, puppy fur?

"I didn't want the spider to land on Mr. Chang," I say.

"But it was a spider, a typical spider—definitely not a black widow. Rick said you saved a bee, but then you go out of your way to kill a spider? It doesn't make sense."

I don't know what to say; I can't tell her it was because I wanted to eat it to see what it knew. I know how people react to that.

She lowers her eyes, staring at her sneakers before asking, "Did you agree to help me with the test because you like me?" Then she looks up.

I feel small beneath her stare, but I don't think she's trying to make me feel this way. And this is when I start babbling. It's like someone has taken control of my mouth, and I can't stop myself. Dog-girl's eyes grow with everything I say, her mouth rounding into an O of surprise. I need to stop, but I can't. I keep blurting stuff. I don't know what to do, but I must do something, so I pluck the ant from her shoulder and crunch it between my molars.

Big mistake. Now I have to hear it all again.

"Did you agree to help me with the test because you like me?"

But now I can see my own face.

I've gone pale, and I meet her eyes. I want to cringe and look away, but even if it were possible, there's something in my stare that holds me, just as it's holding the Dog-girl.

"Do I like you?" I say. "If . . . if I were a praying mantis, I wouldn't mind if you ate me. Not that I think you're mean, or some crazy person that cannibalizes other boys. Lots of bugs eat bugs, right? But not the Graphium agamemnon—have you seen one? They live in the jungle. The caterpillar is green and humpbacked, but then after the metamorphosis, her wings are dappled with emeralds. When I first met you, I thought you were like that butterfly. Your eyes are the same color. I hate tests. I'm terrible at tests. I like . . . bugs. And since you're Dog-girl, I figured, Dog-girl—Bug-boy, you know?"

Crazy.

Then I ate the ant.

When I come to, there is a group around me, and closest of all are those emerald eyes staring down.

"Really? Dog-girl?" she asks, and then walks away, shaking her head.

I miss the test. For once, I would have aced the test, but instead the teacher on lunch duty forces me to go see the vice principal, who tells me to call my mom. My mother wants me home, and it's happened so many times the school lets me go without a parent to pick me up. The whole time in the school office, I'm wondering what Dog-girl thinks of me. So much so that when I pass her locker, I decide to do something drastic. I open my backpack and pull from it the tape and a jar with a spare fly.

Everyone's in class, so no one is around to witness me sticking the fly to the tape, climbing on top of the lockers, and affixing the fly to the ceiling tiles. When I come back I'll be able to eat the fly and listen in on what Dog-girl thinks. Maybe I'll even catch her name.

As I bike home, I do feel ill, but it has nothing to do with bugs or hitting my head. Even I know the fly-cam was wrong. Coming home early gives me time to eat my fly sentries. I unlock the front door and head for my room, the cicada buzzing its alarm. With the door taped back up, I check on all my bugs to ensure they have water and enough to munch on. Then I lie down with my fly tape. I pick a few choice stick bugs off the wall and place them on my chest. I've always felt more comfortable with my pets, but now I feel guilty, wondering how they'll taste.

The room smells like the sort of place where a Graphium agamemnon would fly, fluttering in the humid, musty, rich air.

With the long-legged insects watching over me, I mark down the street number of the first fly and swallow it with a sip of water.

I look in on a completely empty house where no one comes or goes. I can hear the traffic behind me, broken only by the intermittent flitting of wings against the glass. Finally, I come to, but I've learned nothing.

The next moment is at night. Since I nabbed the flies in the morning, I suspect many of them will include a moment at nighttime, but even flies sleep, so this one must have been woken by something. A light flickers across the window, but it's not from a headlight on the road. A flashlight—inside the house. A robber. Despite knowing that this is only a memory, fear trickles down my spine. Something shatters, and the light freezes. Then the flashlight jiggles, racing out of the room.

I catch a profile view of the thief when he goes to shut the light off and turns the beam on his face for a split second. I can't place him. It could be anyone I've seen. Eating that many caterpillars yesterday, I've seen a lot of new people. After the thief disappears, silence returns, broken by the odd car rushing past.

I shudder, and before eating another fly, I take a moment to write a long note about what I saw.

The next home is the woman with the fancy Corvette. Upon swallowing the fly, I see her in a kitchen full of pale greens and yellow-tiled floor.

"Get out!" she screams at a man. "I never want to see you again."

The man, burly and bearded with a baseball cap turned backward, looms over her, and she cowers. Then he seems to crumble into tears until he's kneeling before her.

"But I . . . I think I'm in love with you," he says.

She puts her finger beneath his chin and tilts it up. "Boris, it's over. You snore. And you scratched my car. You scratched my car."

"I'm sorry. I'll cook dumplings. You love my dumplings." He reaches out his hands, palms up, begging.

"Not as much as my car." She shakes her head and walks out of the room while the big guy's shoulders sag.

So that was pretty weird. I feel a bit like a peeping tom. For the second time, I feel as though I'm seeing things I shouldn't be seeing. That I'm stealing from these people as surely as the thief was stealing from that house.

In the next three houses nothing even moves. In the fourth, I spot a shoe behind a floral print couch. If I'd only glanced at it, I wouldn't have thought anything about a discarded shoe, but I am stuck staring into the room with nothing better to do. So, after searching for clues to the trapped dogs, I come back to the shoe—a pink high-heeled shoe. It's tilted at a wrong angle. The toe rests on the floor, but the heel hangs an inch higher—in the air. Which is impossible, unless . . . unless there is a foot in the shoe.

I've passed out enough times to know what my shoe would look like if someone was peering in at me. It would be like this, seeming to float above the floor. I know. I know without a doubt that someone's lying beside the couch. Someone needs Bug-boy's help, and this time I have an address. An opera station plays in the background, and the high-pitched aria grates on me until finally . . .

I'm back on my bed with a stick bug on my nose. "Twig," I say to its waving antennae. "Someone needs my help."

I ignore the two remaining flies and check the address on the last one I ate. After my prior call with the police, there's no way I'm dialing them without more evidence than a fly's memory. I tape the bedroom door, rap my helmet on my head, unlock my bike, and set off to save a life.

Chapter 19
Where Jarrod Breaks the Law

I bang on the front door of passed-out-lady's house. It was one of the homes farthest away from the patch of tar. The small, rundown, end-unit town house has beige paint flaking from its brick walls. A scraggly flower in a planter sits at the front steps. Flyers plaster the porch's cracked concrete floor.

When no one answers, I step through the overgrown lawn and peer in through the window. It's exactly as I'd seen it in my moment. There's something strange about seeing places I've never actually been in reality. The whole being-able-to-eat-a-bug-and-learn-what-it-knows thing is still hard to accept sometimes, even for me.

The shoe is there, floating a bit, tucked to the side of the sofa. But I can't quite tell what it's attached to, no matter my angle at the window. I wish I had brought a roachie.

I knock on the glass. Again, there's no movement. I try the front door, but it's locked. The side door too. I jog around the house to the rear. Its neighboring yard is nicely manicured, but this one has grass nearly to my knees. I suspect someone inside has fallen down and can't get up. If she's dead, she might have

105

been there for a very long time. But if she's alive, she could be dying.

A small window to the side of a sliding door is open a crack. That's my best way in. I pull at the window, trying to reach the crank with my hand. I am stunned when the rotten frame gives way and the whole of it, window and frame, sags out of the house. I whine a little and struggle to hold it up, but it's heavy and I can't keep my grip. I jump out of the way. With a crash, it shatters onto patio stones and sends the local dogs barking.

I clutch my head. Shards of glass are everywhere at my feet. The backs of other townhomes look down on me, but no human has raised the cry of alarm. I want to run away but would feel pretty dumb if I learned later that someone died here.

With not-so-great superpowers come way too much responsibility. I place my palms on the bricks, jump up, slump my chest over where the window had been, and worm my way inside.

It smells rotten, and I cover my mouth with the hem of my T-shirt. I can still get out of here. I look back to the sliding door. No one would blame me for leaving. But I would. I'm better than that.

The floors creak with each step. A cockroach skitters across the floor. I smile at it—it's good to have a friend near. Seeing the roach, I steel myself. The fridge door is open. Maybe someone left it open, or maybe it just gave up and broke. The stench is strongest as I move through the kitchen and into the living room, where opera music plays.

The announcer describes the piece as "having a coruscant melody" that itches at my ears. Flies buzz, but I ignore them. I can't afford to be passed out on the floor.

I step into the living room and stare at the shoe.

It's attached to a leg, only the leg remains—wait

—a woman's leg—wait

—it's a lamp made to look like a woman's leg.

The whole thing is a single piece of pink plastic with an electrical cord running to an outlet. I've tried to save the ugliest lamp ever made.

"Hey!" someone calls.

I look back toward the kitchen and see a dark shadow silhouetted in the empty window hole I created.

"What are you doing in there? I'm calling the cops."

And now I'm a fugitive for having tried to save the ugliest lamp ever made.

"No, I—" And once again I'm confronted with the dilemma. No one will believe me, and no crime has even been committed. Except mine. The only thing that's happened is that I've broken into someone's house. Worse, I ripped an entire window out of it. At this rate, I'll be in jail within the hour.

Someone grunts at the rear, and I imagine the person pulling himself through the window.

Run! And finally, my body responds. I reach the front door and fumble with the lock. The deadbolt snaps free and I throw open the door. Heavy steps thud over the kitchen floor behind me. I slam the door and don't even glance back as I stumble down the steps.

I pick up my bike, run with it, my shins striking pedals, and jump on. I weave across the street right through traffic. Cars honk, but I'm alive as I hit the opposite sidewalk. I pedal furiously, first across the park, and then crisscrossing the neighborhood streets to throw off anyone who could still be following. Finally, hearing no sirens and seeing no signs of pursuit, I tuck into my driveway. I drop the bike on the porch. Once inside, I lean against the front door. With my hands on my knees, I breathe heavily in the cool, dark foyer. The house is silent. My bruised shins ache.

The sofa springs groan, and I straighten. I'm not alone.

"We want to talk to you, Jarrod," my mom says. "Come in and sit down."

My parents are waiting in the living room. Both of them.

This is not good.

Chapter 20
Where Jarrod Is Judged

My mother twists her rings. My dad shifts in the chair beside her. No lights are on, and the light from the windows is fading. They've waited in the dark. They've come home from work early and waited in the dark for me. How did they find out about the break-in so quickly?

I sit on the couch beside my mom. I wish I could sit farther away, but she's patting the cushion as if inviting me to the witness stand.

"We want you to be honest with us," she says, touching me on my thigh. Here we go; I recite in my head, *I promise to tell the whole truth, and nothing but the truth.* "We've had a phone call."

I nod. Something tells me to keep from talking. That anything I say can and will be used against me.

"Mr. Chang called. He's marked the tests."

I collapse into the couch and grin. "Is that all? Is this about missing a test?"

"Did you cheat?" she asks.

I am confused. "Cheat on what? I didn't take the test. I was sick, remember?" My dad shakes his hand at my mom as if to say—*see, that's what I said.* But it's not enough for my mom. And I'm beginning to realize what's happened.

"I know that, but two students in your class received perfect marks, and one of them said you helped her study."

"Oh," I say. And I wonder what Dog-girl's saying about me right now. Is she angry about the fuss I've caused or impressed that I helped her get a perfect mark on her very first test? Somehow, I don't think it's the perfect mark.

"'Oh' is right," my mom says. "Explain this, please."

And my fingers tighten slowly into fists, and my jaw clenches as I realize how little faith my parents have in me. "You don't think I could have helped them without cheating?"

"Answer the question, please." My mom's in total lawyer mode.

"You didn't phrase it as a question." This little comeback hangs in the air. I'm out of my depth. No one wins an argument with my mom. No one.

Her eyes widen a little. "Can you explain to your parents, the judge and jury, why one of your classmates would say that you helped her get a perfect score on a science test?"

I look around the court. In order to hang a jury, the defense only needs to convince one of the jurors of their innocence. My dad stares at me with a mix of pity and the slimmest glimmer of hope. I jut out my chin.

"You know Gavin is a genius. Maybe they are both very good at science," I say. "Even I got an A, remember?"

"No maybe. Answer the question." My mom's eyes are piercing, and I bet she's formidable in court.

I take a deep breath. "I ate a spider that saw the test."

Air whistles out of my dad's nose.

"You cheated," my mom says.

"There is no rule against eating bugs," I reply.

"It's not like we can tell the school any of this," my dad says. "But there would be a rule if they knew."

"Objection," I say. "This isn't fair. How is this different from eating a bug to help sell a car?"

Dad ponders this for a second and shakes his head. "It's very different. I'm helping my customers. I'm trying to figure out what they want. I'm not hurting them, I'm helping them."

"By spying on them to hear what they would never say to your face, then using that information to make sales?" I say. "And what about Mom, then? Did she help anyone but herself and her law firm by grabbing a billion dollars from some other company?"

"It's not the same thing at all," my mother snaps. "The people I'm up against are practically criminals, and that money will also go to people who deserve it. And this isn't about us."

"So, it is okay for me to spy to help you in your jobs, but not to help myself at school?" I ask, knowing I have her. If they can do it, then I can do it too.

"We're not talking about your father and me. We're not on trial here!"

We all listen to the echo of my mom's shout. She smooths her hands down her pants as if gathering herself.

The verdict is in.

"You will go to your room." Her voice is low as she sentences me. "You are grounded. Tomorrow you will tell the teacher that you saw the test and apologize. And . . . I want all of your bugs gone from your room by this weekend. I've already checked with the pet store, and they'll take everything you've got."

I gasp. "Not my bugs. They'll take everything and feed them to lizards!"

I glance to my dad, but he nods agreement. It's unanimous.

"Now," he says.

Chapter 21
Where Jarrod Loses His Thing

Shaking my head, I shuffle to my room and repeat the taping ritual. I wonder why I bother. This isn't fair, and they know it. I heard their hesitation. I caught my mom out. She knows they shouldn't be using my abilities to help cases or sell cars, and that is why she's so mad. She's mad at herself too. I can't let them take my bugs.

I've got a one-line email message from Gavin. *How could you be so stupid?* Tears spring to my eyes.

I stand in the middle of my room and listen. Bugs have always soothed me. They've always cleared my head to help me think. Right now, my mind roils with anger, frustration, and shame.

So, I take out each of my bugs: the praying mantises on my shoulders, a stick bug on my head, roachies hanging on my shirt, and all the other beetles I place on my legs. Ants I leave to their colony, but I let Monkey roam my arm and wrist.

Bedecked in bugs, I shut my eyes and think.

What's bothering me? What *really*?

Soon it comes. The truth of it. The reason why I'm most angry is not because my punishment is unfair or that my parents are hypocrites; it's because, despite being hypocrites, they're right. It's why I felt badly about helping my mom win the case. It's why I don't like sitting in on private conversations even if it's for a good cause. I shouldn't have used my powers to cheat or spy to make my life easier.

What about the fly-cam I have on Dog-girl? Is wanting to know what she likes or how she feels about me a good enough reason to spy? To kill a fly? I shake my head. Spying on her isn't fair either. I am not doing it to save a life. I suppose that is selfish too. Finding my thing isn't enough. It's figuring out what to do with it. As Monkey's tiny legs tickle my flesh, something else grows clear. It's also not fair that my parents want me to get rid of all my bugs. More than ever, they must know what the bugs mean to me.

I have no friends. I'm no hero. I'm grounded. And stupid.

I stroke each roachie and then begin debugging. I release Monkey to get some exercise on the floor. I'll have to set them free. But most of them won't survive the winter. If only I can prove that my superpower is useful for more than just cheating, maybe then they'll let me keep my bugs. Maybe then I can feel better about myself and what I've done. I sit on the bed and see the last two strips of fly tape. Should I? I rub my face and clench my hands. I owe it to their little fly lives.

I pry a fly off the tape and pop it in my mouth. I collapse back on my pillow.

Nothing.

I mean, I'm staring at a painted windowsill. The tape must have twisted or the fly did, because I can't see anything important. There's some bit of fabric shaped into a cone with a strap attached to it, but I don't know what it's for. I can hear movement and someone singing softly.

When I come to, Monkey is sliding up my arm. I ease forward so that I can write down what I saw and heard. I'm humming the tune, and I shake my head to clear it away.

"One more fly, Monkey," I say, placing her back in the terrarium before chow time. If I don't get lucky on this one, I will have to expand my search to the street behind—more bugs. I swallow the fly.

I have it.

The man before me wears long hair down his back and is twirling the tip of his moustache. He's in his mid-thirties, and his tie-dye shirt and coral necklace scream 1960s. Everything in the room is retro, and it reminds me of the colors and decor of the basement from the puppy-mill moment. His TV looks like an egg. Posters on the wall are all psychedelic. There's a lava lamp. And at his feet, a golden retriever. I have it. I missed one important thing, I realize. Every puppy mill needs at least one male dog. They can't all be female dogs.

I sit up. I drill the roachies one more time, impressed at how well they are remembering their training with the exception of Bent. I don't know what to do with him. And then I'm ready. Into a small jar I carefully place the smart roachies, causing them to hiss at me.

"Sorry you have to travel together, little buddies. This is it."

At the bottom of the terrarium, Bent huddles in silence.

It's time for the elite crew to take their positions, but I'm grounded. I can hear the muffled voices of my parents. I need to escape. If I save the dogs, I save my bugs.

Chapter 22
Where Jarrod Gets Caught

Having my bedroom on the first floor has some advantages. I can get out. But my parents can come in at any time and see that I'm not here. What's more important? Saving the dogs, or doing right by my parents? I know the answer. I've thought about telling them, but if they say no, then I'm really stuck. They're more concerned with my secret getting out.

I stuff some clothes under my bedsheets, making a me-shaped lump in the hopes that they'll think I'm sleeping, but I doubt it'll work. It's too early. My bugs are my best defense. My parents hate them and know that if they come in, they'll have to quickly enter and then retape my door to prevent any of the free-range bugs from slipping out. Then they'll be trapped inside with them. My dad hasn't been in my room since the praying mantis incident.

After securing all my buddies, I slide the window open. It opens on the side of the house. The brisk air sends some of my bugs skittering in their terrariums to find places to keep warm.

I heave myself up onto the windowsill. Then I swing my legs over so that they dangle three feet off the ground. I'm hoping to save a basement full of sick dogs and puppies, and all I have to help me are the bugs in my pocket. I'm terrified, my hands slippery with sweat as I shut the window behind me.

The distance between our house and the neighbor's is only ten feet. As gently as possible, my boots crunch into the gravel. I'm in shadow. With the sunshine on the street, no one walking by will have seen me. I walk out as if I should be there and then start jogging. I can't risk my parents seeing me retrieve the bike on the porch, so I'm forced to make my way on foot. By the time I arrive at moustache-man's house, sweat drips from my chin.

It's a nice spot. Two stories with a cedar shingle roof and siding. I remember now that I'd had to climb the lattice near the front window to stick my fly-cam in place. The driveway curves to a garage, something few homes in the area have. Most people are forced to park on the street. A big tree in the front yard offers a little bit of concealment. I walk past twice, spotting two basement windows. I need to creep up to one of them and release a roachie into the basement. Roachie will scramble down the wall, traverse the room, and then climb back up the wall and out the window. I hope. I am not worried whether the cockroach can scale walls. They can cling to ceilings.

I study the house from the park side of the street. No one moves inside or out. I suspect that the moustachioed man is away at work, or delivering some puppy to a new home. When there's a lull in the traffic, with no one coming from either direction, I dash across the street and over the lawn. I've decided to use the far side of the house, hoping that the shade obscures me a bit from the sidewalk.

I drop into the basement window well amongst a collection

of leaves and bits of wrappers. No one shouts anything. I'm good. First, I peer through the window, but due to grime and the dark I can't see anything even after rubbing my side of the pane clean. There's a crack at the bottom of the sill through which a roachie should find its way beneath.

"Okay, buddies, if you want your sugar, you know what you have to do. Who's it going to be?"

I pull one out of the jar. Legs scrabble and antennae flail. Then I set it by the crack and snap my fingers. It hugs the window before finding the opening at the corner. It's in.

Huddled below the top of the window well, I'm hidden and decide that I'm better off waiting it out here in the musty leaves, rather than risk running back and forth across the lawn. Half a block away is the house I broke into, and five doors down, Corvette woman's house. The chance of someone recognizing me is growing. I miss having Gavin, but I'm mad that he called me stupid. I'm not sure I can forgive him for that.

The only things down here with me are bugs, and lots of them. A daddy longlegs creeps over my calf. Daddy longlegs are not actually spiders because they don't have segments. I hold it in my palm as I inspect it. A minute passes. Then another. I listen to bikes cycle by. Kids laughing. And—

Bang!

Something slams against the metal frame of the window well. I scream and jump up. A baseball bat's cocked back, ready for another swing, and moustache-man's knuckles are white as he grips the handle.

"What are you doing, man?" he demands. "You some thief?"

I have my hand up, fingers splayed.

I dropped the daddy longlegs. He takes a fake swing, and I flinch.

Think, think, think!

"I–I'm researching window wells," I say. "What gets collected in them."

"What gets collected in them . . ." he replies; the bat slides an inch lower on his shoulder.

"Yeah," I say. "Like leaves and things like wrappers." He's not buying it. "And like snakes. I've seen lots of snakes and frogs that can't make it out."

"What in the world for, dude?" he asks.

"Um . . . well . . . to make a business doing window well protection kits." I'm pretty impressed with my quick thinking . Maybe people could use something like that. "You never know when you'll stumble into one. Or worse, some little kid. I'm going to design them and patent it."

He lowers the bat so that the tip rests against his foot. Then his face twists in disgust.

"Oh, man," he says, staring past me to his window. "Roaches. Total downer."

Roachie is sauntering across the lower window frame.

I start to crouch to pick Roachie up, but the man hauls me out by the collar and says, "You can't just come hang out in my window well, dude. It's creepy and weird."

"Yes, sir," I say.

Now that we are on the same level, he gets a good look at me, squinting.

"There've been some break-ins," he says as I back off the lawn. "You don't know anything about them, do you?"

I shake my head. When I reach the sidewalk, I stop and look back. The guy's staring at me, waiting. But I can't leave Roachie. He lifts the bat threateningly. I start to jog home. I guess I wouldn't have made a very good army officer. I am supposed to follow a motto like *leave no roachie behind.*

At my house, I climb back through my window, fall to the floor and shut my eyes.

That could have gone better. I pull the remaining two elite roachies from their jar in my pocket and give them some sugar in their cage. Bent skitters over, happy to share, making me wonder once more whether he's smarter than the others or stupid like me.

"Sorry about your friend," I say. "He'll be okay. Maybe he'll even have fun being missing in action." But I know how misunderstood cockroaches are. He's likely to be stomped on. Four days have passed, and I still haven't saved the dogs.

That night, I go about my chores, eat dinner, and even do a little homework. The whole time I can't stop thinking of the dog's festering sores. It takes a day for flies to lay their eggs and have them hatch. The dog will have maggots on its wound. On the plus side, larvae are good at helping clean wounds. Some doctors still use maggots to eat dead flesh.

I don't know what else to do. Was moustache-man the puppy mill owner? The prospect of sticking up more fly-cams makes me gag. I can't eat another bug. I just can't. I go to bed, trying not to think about those puppies, but all I dream about is the sightless dog.

The next morning, I wake up with a roach on my chin.

Chapter 23
Where Jarrod Swallows His Pride

"Roachie?" I ask its waving antennae.

I lean forward, and it topples from my chin into my palms. "You're so smart!" I glance over to the cockroach terrarium and count three bugs, confirming the impossible.

"You came back," I say. "You actually found your way here!" It's hard to believe, but my roachie must have scurried all night to reach home. Sure enough, at the base of the door a flap of tape has been pushed back. "You're so smart. You're the king of all roachies." I pat it, nearly bursting with pride.

"Oh, oh," I exclaim. "Now, I have to eat you."

My roachies are big and as long as my thumb. I hadn't really considered the best way to eat one. I'm going to need to chew, and I won't be able to fry it up, not with my parents hanging around. I open the door and listen. The shower's running, and Dad must have already left for work. The shower shuts off, but I'll still have time while my mom changes and blow-dries her hair.

I jog into the kitchen and open the fridge. Mayo and roach? Pickled roach? Cheese and roach? Surprisingly, nothing seems to go well with cockroach. Then I spot the peanut butter. I put Roachie down on the chopping board. It tries to crawl away, but I sprinkle some sugar and it stops to eat. How best to kill it? Roaches are hard to kill. Anyone who has tried to squish one knows that a single stomp from a boot heel often isn't enough.

"I'm really sorry, Roachie," I say with my hand clenched above it. So far, I've only eaten stranger bugs, but Roachie's my friend. And I'm not even sure I'll see anything useful given how long it's been.

I knew my roachies were like kamikaze fighters, preparing to give their lives for me, but that doesn't make it easier. Roachie scuttled all night to return home, and the thanks he gets is a quick death? It doesn't seem fair.

I squinch my eyes shut and pound the roachie with a meat tenderizer. I crushed its side, and now it scoots around in circles.

"Oh, no," I say, seeing it in pain. I need to end this—fast. I grab the big meat cleaver. I keep my eyes open for this one and aim for the neck.

Thwack. Thwackity-thwack!

The head comes away, but the body, it keeps moving. I've heard about this—they are *really* tough to kill. Footsteps are coming down the hall. My mom.

I spin off the peanut butter lid and drool peanut butter over the bug parts, then I scoop it up and shove it, head and body, into my mouth. You never really know where the brain is—some grasshoppers have ears on their legs—and I don't want to do this twice. My mother walks into the kitchen.

I still feel it twitching on my tongue.

"What are you doing?" she asks.

I shake my head. Nothing.

"You nervous about talking to Mr. Chang?"

I hadn't even thought about that. I bite down, and then try to swallow, but with all the peanut butter it's not going anywhere. I gag a little, race to the fridge, pull out the milk carton and drink from the spout.

"Ugh, gross, I don't care how badly you need a drink. Never do this," my mom says.

Then I hit the floor. *Forgot about that.*

I'm in the basement, on my way out. I've waited too long to eat Roachie. It's climbing the concrete wall toward the window. Luckily, behind me I can see the stainless-steel furnace and piles of crates, skis, windsurfers, scuba gear, and no giant box. I don't need to see the rest of the journey, but on I march home, only taking the odd break as I catch glimpses of streets and narrow misses from cars, even a screeching woman who fails to hit Roachie with her stiletto-heeled shoes. Roachie is much, much faster than I would have thought. He slept in my room most of the night before climbing up onto my chin.

Then I'm looking at my mom again.

"You're back, thank heavens," she says and strokes the side of my head. "That was a long one. I almost called the ambulance. What did you eat?"

I look over. Almost half an hour has passed. Roachies are the dolphins of the bug world.

"Peanut butter," I say. She straightens and tosses the whole container in the garbage.

"Told you that you need your helmet still. Bugs are everywhere." She shudders and rubs her arms. "Are you okay to go to school on your own? You'll be late again."

I nod, and she grabs a banana before heading out to her scooter. I'm having a hard time concentrating. If the moustachioed man isn't the puppy mill owner, then who is? I'm out of bugs!

At school, I'm glad I'm late. It costs me a late slip but allows me the time and privacy I need to scrape the fly off the ceiling above Dog-girl's locker. I suppose I could have just left it there, but it doesn't seem right to leave the bug in place. I'd be prolonging its misery and that isn't fair. I fold the taped fly into my wallet and head to class. I will not eat the fly. I owe Dog-girl that much. But I'm not quite ready to throw it away either. She's covered in dog fur all the time. She smells like dogs. Maybe, just maybe, she's somehow connected with the puppy mill, and the pet store clue she gave me was a red-herring. If so, I will need all the evidence I can get.

Mr. Chang works his tongue around in his cheek as I enter and take my seat. I'd almost forgotten about the test. Dog-girl stares stiffly at the whiteboard without even a glance at me. On the whiteboard are drawings of all the parts of a flower. I redraw them in my notebook but barely take in what Mr. Chang teaches. At the end of class, Dog-girl turns away, collects her things, and walks off. So, this hasn't been a positive development in our relationship. By the look of Gavin, it hasn't been one in ours either.

He glowers as he walks up to my desk.

"I've never failed anything. You shouldn't have told her too. One of us getting perfect would have been believable, but two?" Gavin asks out of the side of his mouth. So, Gavin's mad because I told people who weren't him?

Mr. Chang clears his throat.

"Gavin, I'd like to talk to Jarrod, thank you," Chang says, sliding onto Dog-girl's desk.

When the last student has exited the class, Mr. Chang pulls out the proofs I gave to Dog-girl and then gives me a thin-lipped smile that's apparently my invitation to speak.

"I saw the question on your desk," I say.

Mr. Chang shakes his head. "No. The test went from my pocket to the desk, but only for a moment and then back to my pocket. I made copies right before the test and handed them out myself. No one had the chance to read the test on my desk."

I shrug.

"If you're protecting someone, you shouldn't," he says.

I nod. So that's what he thinks. That someone who took the test last year told me what was on the test.

"My best guess is Gavin's sister told him," he adds. "If that's the truth, then you won't be in trouble."

"I didn't ask anyone or hear from anyone. I saw it on your desk," I say.

Chang turns and peers from where he sits, to his desk, and then looks up to where I smacked the spider. His mouth works back and forth, and then he shrugs. "I don't know how you did it, but not only did you get the test question in advance, you also tricked two other students into cheating. I don't know how, and no one is explaining, so you will all have detention. Today at three thirty."

"Mr. Chang," I say. "They didn't know I was giving them the question. It wasn't their fault."

His jaw tightens. "If I can't trust you to tell me how you

learned the question, then I can't trust anything you're saying."

I nod and get up to leave.

"Jarrod?" he asks.

I pause.

"Do you know why I placed you in Gifted this year?"

I shake my head.

"Because I believed in you."

Chapter 24
Where Jarrod Loses a Friend

For detention, Mr. Chang splits us up, and I've been ordered to sit at the front of the class. Dog-girl's in the middle, and Gavin is in the back. Chang says, "No talking. No moving." I can feel Dog-girl's eyes drilling into my spine.

"There are dogs that need to pee because of you," Dog-girl whispers. She shakes something and slams it down on the desk.

Mr. Chang pokes his head into the class, glaring at each of us. "No talking," he says.

I wait until his footsteps echo down the hall. I want to tell her that some dogs might be dying right now because of this. Because of me, but I don't.

"I didn't mean . . . I didn't want anyone to get into trouble. I'm sorry," I say.

"Thank you," Gavin says.

"I'm not as sorry about you," I reply.

"What? You gave her my work!" he says in a harsh whisper. "*My* work."

"You knew you were cheating," I say.

"Yes, but when you didn't show for the test, I thought I was cheating alone. I've never cheated. You've corrupted me," he says. "It's not the same for you. I've never seen an F before."

I turn in my chair to yell at him and then see what Dog-girl slammed down on the desk.

"What's that?" I ask, pointing at a collection of leashes, key chains, and poop bags.

"What?" she replies, chin up and threatening. "My dog walking stuff?"

"No, that. The black thing." Looped into the handle of a pink leash is the same black mesh cone-thing I stared at while listening to the humming-woman during my moment.

"A muzzle. It keeps one of the dogs from biting the other dogs."

I look meaningfully at Gavin, but he's oblivious to the discovery. Does she just happen to have the same muzzle? Is the house with the muzzle the puppy mill? I've been by that house five times now. They have no dog, so why do they own a muzzle?

Gavin shakes his head. "You don't think she's running the puppy mill, do you?"

He speaks in a stage whisper that I know she can hear because her eyes grow big and round.

"*What*? What are you talking about? I *love* dogs. I love dogs like you love bugs." She shoots to her feet, her chair's legs screeching over the floor. "A puppy mill? What are you talking about?"

"I didn't say it. Gavin did," I reply. Both my hands are up, trying to coax her back down.

"You were thinking it," Gavin says.

"Now you're so smart that you know what I'm thinking?" I demand.

He rolls his eyes.

"I know where it is," I say. "We have to go."

"I'm not getting into more trouble," he says, folding his arms against his chest.

"What are you talking about? None of this makes any sense. Will someone explain it to me?" Dog-girl demands.

"Whatever. I'll go. It's more important than detention," I say. "I guess I'm just stupid."

"The least you can do is give me an explanation," she says. "You're going to get into such trouble."

"Sometimes you have to do what you have to do, even if it's going to hurt," I say. I peek through the classroom door and then turn back. "I really am sorry you both got in trouble."

As I leave, I hear her say to Gavin, "You're going to tell me what's going on, if it's the last thing you do."

And then I'm out where the janitor is waxing the floors. He can probably tell from my furtive look that I'm up to no good. He winks and slowly turns the polisher so that his back is to me. Then he cranks it up, the machine sounds covering my footsteps as I run down the hall. Outside, I lean on my bike, breathing heavily. It's four o'clock. With any luck, I have enough time to fetch my roachies and investigate the humming-person's house. One more hour until most people return home from work.

A hand grabs my shoulder.

"Jarrod." It's Mr. Chang. The crushing look of disappointment on his face yanks down the corners of my mouth.

"I'm sorry, Mr. Chang, I know I'm going to be in more trouble. But I have to leave. I have to. You wouldn't understand."

"Why do you think I wouldn't understand?" he asks. "Try me."

I pause. It's not like telling him the truth can land me in any more trouble.

"I learned what was on the test because I ate a spider that saw it."

"The spider above my desk," he says. "It wasn't a black widow then."

I nod and say, "If I eat bugs I can learn what they saw."

He smooths down his white cowlick, but it pops back up again. "Let me get this straight. You wanted to know what was on the test, so you faked that there was a dangerous spider. Ate it . . . absorbed its memories and then told your friends."

I don't even move.

"That's remarkable," he says. "I've never heard of anything of the sort."

I cough. "You . . . you believe me?"

"Should I have reason to doubt you?" His dark eyes burn with challenge.

"No, sir."

"So, you did cheat. You used your . . . power to cheat. And, therefore, you owe me a detention."

"I do, but I can't," I say. "I can't stay. I'll do ten detentions later. Whatever you want."

Chang folds his arms across his chest. "And why is that?"

"I swallowed a fly and learned that there's a puppy mill somewhere, with dying dogs. I think I know where it is."

He blinks and takes a step back, unfolding his arms and pointing.

"Then Jarrod, my boy, you must go! What are you waiting for? Go! Go and save those dogs."

And then he pushes me so that I get a quick start on my bike. Pedaling into the bright sunlight, I puff my chest out, give my head a shake in wonderment. And then, as if buoyed by Mr. Chang's belief in me, I bike harder than I ever have in my life.

Chapter 25
Where Jarrod Eats One Bug Too Many

Humming-woman's house has a single story and a well-tended front garden with trimmed bushes and bright fall flowers, including huge trellises of fading roses. A maple has shed a carpet of leaves. Aside from a few parents pushing strollers, who won't think anything of a boy playing in a driveway, there aren't many people walking past. Cars buzz by quickly. I sit on warm pavement. Not cobblestone. My legs hang in the window well.

I had to return home to pick up my roachies. I bottled them all, even Bent, and brought the packets of ketchup my mom started buying so I can eat everything bug free. Now I'm using the packets to wash down bugs. With any luck, this is all going to be over soon. In half an hour, I'll call in the cavalry and Bug-boy will be a true superhero. I smile off into the distance and then shake my head clear as a runner passes the house. First, I have to prove myself. To everyone.

I can't wait any longer. I'm upset Gavin's not here, though. I need him. I worry about passing out for half an hour alone, and I don't have time to go back home after a roachie does its job. If I do, my parents will catch me for sure. It's dark on the other side of the pane of glass, and the sunlight glares brightly from the window, making it difficult to see inside. It is open a crack, however, and I prepare to send in my roachie.

I place it at the windowsill and snap my fingers. It scoots around the base of the window well but doesn't find the way inside. I sigh, but I was ready for this. I brought along a jar of nail polish so that I can paint the roachies I use, put a dab of pink on its carapace so that I can tell which is which after I return it to the jar. I put a pink dot on its back and return it to its friends. Then I pull out a new roachie, place it right at the corner of the gap in the window, and snap my fingers again.

After watching the roachie slip inside, I stand and look around the park.

Creak, creak. Creak, creak. Some swinging kid rattles my nerves.

I can't stop shivering despite the warmth of the sun. Wind rustles leaves, shaking them loose from branches. The scent of fresh cut grass wafts over me. So many normal things feel weird when I know that somewhere in this neighborhood animals are trapped, sick, and suffering.

By the time I return to the house, it's only been five minutes. I don't want to miss my roachie and then have it start ambling back home.

From the sidewalk, I see the flash of carapace, but a jogger's coming, and I peer into the boughs of a tree while he passes. Then I run up the driveway with the roachie moseying toward me. Dine in or eat out? I have to decide. Eating roachies isn't easy. Not with all the shards and sticky-outy bits. If I go home and my parents catch me, they'll never let me leave again.

Dine in.

I stomp three times. It would have been nice to have chosen somewhere where I wouldn't then have to eat the gravel stuck to it, but I'm not thinking straight. I could be twenty feet from the dogs! I am finishing this now, with or without Gavin. I pick up the dead roach.

I sprint for the park and hide within a big, orange, plastic tube on the top of the play structure. A safe place to have a moment, even a long one. Lying flat with my sneakers sticking out of one end, I tear open the package of ketchup and squeeze it into my mouth. With a fingernail, I scrape off the worst of the gravel and place the bug on my tongue. There's no milk to chug, no water to down, so I need to chew well to ensure I don't choke on the fragments of exoskeleton. That's the hardest part. It is like eating a lobster with the shell included.

The first bite has a crunch to it. With the second, its insides explode into my mouth. I can't say it tastes good. I taste ketchup, asphalt, and something a little like I'd imagine is near enough to toilet water. My stomach heaves. I need to gobble it down before I barf. So much for chewing.

I try to swallow, but I can't. I have a piece of wing or an antenna or some legs caught at the back of my throat. My chest heaves as I choke. I scramble out of the tube and topple down the slide. At the park fountain I press the button, but they've already shut the water down for winter. I gag. Can't breathe.

I recall a hose wheel on the side of humming-woman's driveway. I run for the hose. I only need a sip. As I hold my mouth shut, I twist the tap on and stuff the end of the hose between my lips. The water surging into my mouth has stewed in the hose for a long time. It's hot from the sun and tastes of rubber. But it tastes better than cockroach. The water pressure forces a great swallow and then I'm on the pavement, lying in the middle of the driveway.

I can do nothing but watch.

I spend some time bouncing in the jar with my roachie buddies. Then my hand is setting Roachie down beside the crack in the window, and I slip down the wall. The only things I see are some boxes—one's marked "Christmas Decorations" and another "Halloween." Then I'm on top of them and curling down the side of the cardboard onto a shag carpet floor. And then I see it. The great white box covered with all sorts of puffy soundproofing and a thick metal door. Seeing it, knowing it to be so close, I wrestle with my moment, struggling to wake up. I'm lying in the middle of the driveway of a sicko. But I can't move. Not until the memory has run its course. And roachie memories are long ones.

On the roachie travels, struggling through the heavy carpeting, lumbering to stop in first one corner, snuffling about as if confused by the lack of sugar before marching on to the next. In this corner is a small bathroom, and I imagine the dogs may be allowed out to be bathed every so often before returning to their cages. But I know deep down that the mother dogs have never been out and never will be, not without my help. Roachie dutifully inspects the bathroom before moving on.

Now I can see the other side of the box. Heavy cushions are strapped tight to the walls of this side as well. We hug stairs leading to the ground floor. At the final corner, the roachie stops and takes a moment to rest or to search out the nonexistent sugar before sauntering off, up the boxes, and then the wood-panelled wall to the window. I can almost sense its excitement for sugar. Its belief in me. Back in the sunlight, I crush it.

Suddenly, I'm staring into the deep brown eyes of a dog. Their wells of despair are worse than the bulbous red polyp rising from its brow.

I recognize the cages. I'm in the puppy mill. But Roachie didn't go in there. Roachie had searched the perimeter of the basement like it was supposed to. Hadn't it? So why am I staring at the dog? The smell of their feces hits me. I move my head, and of course, if I'm in a moment, I'm not in control of the vision and shouldn't be able to move my head. I shut my eyes. And reopen them. This isn't a moment anymore.

I scream.

I'm trapped with the dogs, caged in the basement. The puppy mill owner moved me while I was collapsed on the driveway.

The dogs start barking too. And finally, there's a banging on the door followed by a muffled, "Stop your barking, or I'll give you something real to whimper about."

And the dogs stop so suddenly, even the puppies, that I decide maybe I'd better shut up as well.

Chapter 26
Where Jarrod Calms Down

The dog stares at me from its cage, across a two-foot space. I'm on my knees, curled into a ball, with my arms out and fingers threaded through silver bars. I try to straighten but hit the top of my cell. I'm trapped. I could be here for years. The walls of the prison start to close in on me. And then I realize I'm hyperventilating. I'm in trouble, real trouble.

I try to slow my breathing, but I see no reason *not* to be terrified. Except. Except it won't help me escape. But my parents will save me, right? They'll find out I left detention and come looking for me. But where will they look? I purposefully left no note so they couldn't stop me. Maybe Gavin will know where to look? Either he'll remember the house with the humming-woman and rosebushes, or he'll know to use the address book with my notes. He's smart. Really smart. And my parents are sure to ask him. Eventually. But that could be hours from now. And hours before they find the solution . . .

I gulp. If my parents don't know where to look and if they don't ask Gavin soon, they may not find me before it's too late. Where did I put the addresses? It's still on my bed. But I'd had a map of the street's houses in my pocket. I feel for it now. It's missing. Scrawled across the top had been *Potential Puppy Mills.*

The police may not even start looking for a couple of days. They would never believe a bug-eating story, and I'd had a fight with my parents. They'll probably think I ran away, hid out down by the river. If I'm to escape soon, it'll be on my own.

Breathe, I tell myself. *Breathe . . . I can do this. I can.*

The cages come back into focus. Puppies start to yip and are moving around and tumbling over one another. They look healthy enough, but there's a one-eyed dog and another with a sore all down its foreleg. All their fur is matted, and most of them stare at me miserably, except the blind dog that's no longer moving. The mommy-dogs have no room to stand. They've been down here a long, long time, maybe their whole lives. Flies buzz about.

A muscle cramps in my leg, but I don't have the room to straighten it.

I bang my hand against the metal. The cage door rattles but doesn't budge. Something drips on me from above. At least three other cages rise atop mine. I glance up to see the source of the drip; a string of yellow goo drizzles from above and I start to panic again.

Get it together.

The door mechanism is two metal bars on springs that I need to squeeze together to open. When I try, neither move. I shift forward in my prison to glance up and discover a heavy brass lock snapped around the top bar.

I start to hyperventilate again and force my breathing to slow. Why would a dog cage have a lock? Maybe I'm not the first person to discover this little operation.

What am I going to do?

But before I can do anything, there comes a sound at the door.

"Is my new puppy hungry?" asks the voice through the steel.

The other dogs perk up enough to lift their heads before slumping back down. One whines, but the puppies yip with delirious joy.

The door opens, and in the door frame stands my captor.

The humming-woman smiles pleasantly at me, wearing a knee-length skirt dress like those I've seen on old *Star Trek* reruns. Her hair is stacked in a giant beehive, and her face heavily made up with bright blue eye shadow above false lashes. This is a woman who never advanced past the larval stage.

"How are my puppies?" she asks and makes kissy sounds.

"Let me go," I say.

"You should be having fun with all the puppies. I can tell, you know. If you're having fun."

She says this last without a trace of a smile. And I know that I'm being watched.

"Let me go."

But she ignores me, popping the lid off a bucket and scooping dry kibble from it. The puppies yammer away. Dozens of cute, fuzzy, yellow puppies snuffle at their bars while their mothers don't have the room to stand.

"Oh, you love me, don't you? Of course, you do." Tiny pink tongues loll between bars to lick her.

The woman steps toward me. From my lowest of all cages, I can count the stubble on her legs. I can smell her sugary perfume. Dog food scatters to the floor as she feeds the dogs above me.

A dog growls and snaps; at least one dog still has fight in her.

"Do you want me to get your muzzle, naughty doggy?" she admonishes, and there's the snap of metal bars falling back into place.

"Let me go?" I ask. "I promise not to tell."

She crouches down. She smiles at me, but any pretense of kindliness has gone. "You just got here, little doggy. Do you really want it to be *over*?"

Without unlocking the cage, she starts dropping kibble through the bars.

"What's your name, my pup?"

"Jarrod," I say, seeing no reason to lie. "I won't tell anyone. I wouldn't." *Plink, plink,* goes the dog food. "You're not expecting me to eat this, are you?"

"Oh, I don't know what to do with you," she says as if to herself. "I try to sell my puppies. But I can't keep the ones I can't sell. Especially the boys. They're no good to me."

I swallow.

"My parents know where I am," I say, but my voice lacks conviction. The woman flashes another smile before baring all her teeth.

"You know, Jarrod, every litter has its differences, but they also have their similarities." She opens a cage and pulls out a docile little pup that mewls in her hand. "There's always a runt, see. This boy likely won't survive. He can't get enough milk. Can't fight for kibble." Her hand disappears again, and from her fingers dangles a roly-poly puppy. "Now this here's the bully. He gets his share and then some." Its legs scrabble in the air, and it opens its snout to reveal needle-sharp teeth that nip for her hand.

"Who deserves to live more, do you think? The runt or the bully? Who will succeed? Surely it makes sense for the strong one to survive." She grins. "Easy decision, isn't it, when you think of it that way." Her hands squeeze the fat puppy until it whines.

She's the strong one here. She's the one in control. "Should I even bother letting the runt try when I know no one will ever love him, will ever see him? Why do we even bother letting it try?" Her eyes return to mine. "You're a runt too, aren't you, Jarrod?"

Angry tears fill my eyes, and I look away from her clownish features. When my eyes are clear, she's gone. And it's dark in my prison.

She's right. I'm stupid. I'm like Bent. I'm the runt.

Chapter 27
Where Jarrod Paints a Roach

For the next hour, I shout myself hoarse. I bang on the cage. I scream for help. All I do is send the puppies yipping. I've seen the padding around this room. It's soundproof, and what little sound might escape probably won't make it past the walls of the basement. More fluid has leaked on me from above, so my shirt is wet and I smell like everything in here.

Light outside of the box emanates beneath the heavy steel door, allowing me to see.

I can't tell how much time has passed. Gavin should be home by now. My parents will be home by now and wondering what happened to me. I hope.

A shadow pauses before the dull light beneath the door, and I catch my breath. Is she coming to finish me? But there's another voice, a voice asking questions. It's muffled by the door, but as it grows louder and closer, I recognize it. Gavin!

"Wait a second, you're not a nice person, are you?" I can picture him seeing the box in the middle of the room. His mind whirling as to what it might be for, recalling my description of my moment . . .

"Run, Gavin!" I shout. "Run."

"You have my friend," he says. "Hey—"

The door slams open, and Gavin is shoved inside so hard that he crashes against the cages and falls backward, hitting his head on the floor.

"Gavin," I call to him, but he's dazed.

"Ridiculous runts, what do you think you're doing?" the woman says, as if we've done something wrong. "What am I supposed to do with you? How did you find me? Hmm?"

Genuine distress twists over her face. She can't let us go, but she's forced to deal with us somehow.

She opens another low cage, kitty-corner to mine, and starts shuttling the puppies in it into the one beside it. This one's already full, so she has to stuff them in and quickly shut the cage before they all fall out. Then she crams Gavin into the puppy-free cage full of urine-soaked newsprint. In his stupor, he goes easily, and soon his cage door is barred and locked as well.

Then she leaves, still mumbling about runts and getting rid of them.

"Gavin, Gavin, are you okay?" I say when the door shuts.

He groans. "Yeah . . . I think so, but no, I'm so not okay. She's going to kill us."

A warmth suffuses my stomach when I realize something.

"You came for me," I say. "You came to find me even though you said you wouldn't."

He scoffs. "Yeah, too bad I'm an idiot and walked right into a trap. She told me you'd hit your head and were inside on the couch. There's another problem too. No one else knows. Not where we are."

I shut my eyes.

"Well . . . thanks."

"Don't thank me yet."

"We have to get out of here," I say. "But there's a camera."

Gavin rattles his door.

"There's a lock on your cage and mine," I say.

"What do you have? Anything on you?" Gavin asks. "She took my phone, and I didn't have anything else useful."

I take an inventory. I have a belt. I have clothes. I have nail polish and my two remaining roachies. She left my wallet, but there's nothing useful in there.

"I have an idea," I say.

"What, what is it?" he asks. I hear the desperation in his voice.

"I don't want to say. If there's a camera in here, it might have a microphone."

He shuts up. I bet it's hard for him. The truth is, my idea's so dumb I don't want to say it aloud.

I fish the nail polish out of my pants and open the bottle. I pull my remaining roachies from my pocket. Here's my plan. It's a long shot, but I hope that one of these will make their way home and into the sightline of my parents.

I don't waste any time and twist the cap off the nail polish. I need to keep the roachies well back from the bars for fear of the woman spying them from wherever she has her cameras. I try to look casual and keep testing the bars because I figure she'd expect me to at least try to escape. Then I begin to write on the cockroach. Writing on such a small surface that's trying to crawl away isn't easy. And at first, I try to write too much. Instead of:

Help me, I'm at 89 Mapleview Avenue. I end up with: *Help.*

And even that's smudged and blurred with the pink dot already on its back. Maybe I can scratch the message in with my belt buckle?

As I try to clean the roachie with my shirt so that I can try again, the bug slips from my grip and scurries out of the cage, where it starts the circuit of the room.

"Oh, no," I say.

Gavin squints out of his cage. With bright pink smeared across its back, the cockroach looks like a giant moving fingernail. I can't reach it; I don't even want to try for fear of calling too much attention to it.

"That's your plan?" he asks, his eyes tracking the cockroach. "I'm going to die."

One more to go. I have to make it count. Then I realize it's Bent, and I clench my eyes shut in disappointment. When I open them, Bent's staring up at me.

"I was going to be famous," Gavin hollers, and I can hear the crazed panic in his voice. "Do you realize what I wanted to be? Really wanted to be?"

I'm about to tell him to shut up, but then realize he could be distracting the woman.

"What?" I ask him, having decided to stick with the nail polish.

"A chef," he says. "I love food. Love it."

I'd never known he wanted to be a chef. I always figured a doctor or a lawyer, maybe a scientist. But I can't think and write at the same time.

SOS-89 Mapleview. It's still too much, and the polish doesn't wipe easily, but I manage to rub it clean so that I can start again.

Gavin starts yammering away about everything on his list. The seven wonders of the natural world he wanted to visit before he died. The languages he'd planned on learning. Skydiving. Scuba diving. Cliff jumping. It sounds as though he hasn't really figured out his thing after all.

The dog across from me stares, and I wonder if I really do glimpse interest—hope—before going back to painting Bent. This time, I hold the roachie tight and use a single hair of the brush to deliver a neat inscription.

89 MV. I manage at last. And I'm done. I can only hope that if my parents see a painted bug they'll know I'm trying to tell them something. Gavin's gone quiet. I release the roachie, and the bug scoots out of the cage and then turns to stare as if waiting for a signal. I snap my fingers. It doesn't move. I sense the lens of the crazy woman's camera.

Bent meets my eye.

"You can do this, Bent," I whisper. "I . . . I believe in you."

Watching the last roachie exit, Gavin says, "Please, someone help us."

He lapses into silence.

There's nothing left for me to do but wait.

I find myself staring off in a daze, everything a bit too much to take in. Time passes, maybe another hour. We don't talk. The only light is from a single naked bulb hanging from wires at the ceiling. There's a knock on the door, and the woman doesn't wait for an answer before sweeping in.

"Look, puppies," she says. "Jarrod brought a dessert of his own for us to share, isn't that nice?"

I glance up. Something cold gapes in my stomach like the

maw of a deep ocean fish. On the plate lies a cockroach. A dead painted cockroach. I can see how the roachie died, stomped upon, likely by one of the sharp heels of her shoes. I hope it died quickly.

I try hard to keep the look of hope off my face, but part of me cannot. Although I mourn the loss of my roachie, part of me wants to cheer—it didn't die in vain. There's only one on the plate. The second roachie escaped. Bent has left the building.

Chapter 28
Where Jarrod Is the Sidekick

Psst!

I groan and hit my head on the cage roof. Somehow, I fell asleep.

Psst! "Jarrod."

It's late. The middle of the night.

Now I understand what woke Gavin. She's banging around upstairs. She can't be up to any good.

Something else has changed though. It's quiet in here.

"The puppies," Gavin says. "They're gone."

"She's leaving—escaping," I say.

"Leaving us to rot."

"We need to get out of here," I reply. "We can't wait any longer."

"Wait until she's gone."

"Then she'll escape."

"So? At least we'll be alive. Someone will find us *eventually*."

A dog whines. She left the mommy dogs. Discarded them like garbage. If I let the woman go, she'll do this again in another neighborhood, in another city. I know it.

"No, I'm stopping her."

"How?" he asks.

"We have to break out."

"Shh . . . the camera."

"I don't think we have time to worry about the camera," I reply. "These cages are thin wire. They're not made to withstand huge forces. I can do it."

"And you are huge forces?" he asks.

"With my helmet, I'm like a juggernaut." On my head is perhaps my greatest asset, and I'd forgotten all about it.

"When?"

Now.

I brace my feet against the rear of the cage, which abuts the wall. The theory is that when I lunge forward, my helmet will smash into the cage door and bend it. Hopefully enough to break the door open.

I'm cramped. My knees are bent, and I'm holding the cage door with my fingertips. I feel a leg spasm coming on.

"One, two, three," I count before pushing out with my legs. I hit the center of the cage door, but it doesn't swing free.

"Come on, Bug-boy!" Gavin cheers as quietly as he can.

I held back a bit. I shouldn't have. Upstairs, the sounds have stopped.

I don't want her coming back while I'm caged. The crazy woman sees us as troublesome runts that need to be put down.

Footsteps above run across the floor. With my knees tucked and braced again, I lunge forward and slam into the bars. The door bows outward, the bottom portion hanging free of the slot that holds it locked.

She's on the basement stairs.

I rear back as the door to the room opens, then I spring, crashing head-on into the wire mesh. The cage breaks. I'm free. The woman screeches. The dogs bark again. She stands before me, but she's not looking at me, instead at the tower of cages above me that I've shifted away from the wall in my efforts. She screams. The dogs topple forward in their cages.

She groans under the weight of them, holding them up with her shoulder. I duck back inside my cage and kick out again. The sudden lurch is too much for her. The cages crash down. Other pens open in the mayhem, sending dogs out across the floor. But they only whimper and cower.

"Run, Jarrod," Gavin screams. "Save yourself!"

The woman struggles beneath a twisted cage. I crawl out of mine and then stop to pull at Gavin's door, but of course he's locked in.

"What are you doing? Get out of here!" Gavin shouts.

After the hours in the confined space, my legs are stiff and sore. I quake like the dogs. I stumble for the door, but then her hand catches my ankle. I kick out, but she rolls to hold on with both hands.

"Come here, you little runt," she says.

And instead of running or screaming or doing anything that seems sane at all, I dive back toward her, landing on her, helmet first, with hands closed into fists. The breath whooshes out of her chest.

There's a crash upstairs, but I barely register it. She grows frantic, scrambling to stand.

"Police," someone shouts. I don't have breath to call for help, but Gavin does.

"Help! In the basement!" he yells.

She screeches.

"How'd you find me, kid?" she demands. "How?"

"Choked on a bug," I say.

I stand between her and the door. She pulls a short knife from her pocket. With a grunt, she stabs for me. Something snarls, and then a dog hangs from her forearm, worrying at her wrist. She cries out and lashes at it. My helmet digs into the woman's stomach and deflects a swipe from the knife. She flies back and stumbles over the strewn cages, but recovers to slice downward with the blade. I narrowly dodge it and fly into the mess of dogs as she breaks for the door.

I snatch out to hold on to her ankle, trying to draw her back.

"Get her, hold her," Gavin cries, rattling the bars of his cage.

A heel of her shoe catches my hand, and she breaks loose. She's headed for a basement window and has already slid it open by the time I reach the shag carpet. I'm going to be too late, but that's when a dog lopes across the floor and bites her ankle.

Her eyes grow wide as she kicks at the dog. She stares at me, beyond me, and suddenly hands grab my shoulders. And I'm carried backward.

"Police!" someone shouts.

I let the officer carry me to the stairs. A second officer mashes a knee into the small of the woman's back and cuffs her. Her hair has sprung free of its hive and hangs in long tresses that remind me of snakes.

The door to the outside slaps open, and the cool rush of night flows over me. I'm going to be all right. The dogs are safe. Gavin will be safe.

The cop helps me through the door into the back of the cruiser. I wouldn't have thought I needed help, but my legs have gone rubbery. A second police car arrives, lights flashing. Neighbors have emerged from front doors and stare on as the puppy-mill lady is pulled from the house and shoved into the other vehicle. I am trying to speak, to tell them about Gavin.

"You, okay, son?" the cop asks from the front of the car.

"My friend's in there," I say.

A few minutes later, Gavin emerges and sits on the car seat next to me. In his hands is the dead roachie. I thank him and put it in my pocket. A good superhero buries his sidekicks. No bug left behind.

"Are you Jarrod?" the other cop asks. "The kid with the bug trick?"

"Can't believe it worked," Gavin says.

"Yep," I say, guessing that they're talking about Bent.

"The bug-lady's sure to love this one," the cop says to her partner.

"I'm Gavin," Gavin says. "In case you were wondering."

In the cruiser they ask all sorts of questions, and I try to decide whether to tell them the truth or not. In the end, it doesn't seem to matter.

"But how did you *know* about the puppy mill?" one of the cops asks.

"I swallowed a bug and it told me," I admit, ignoring the sharp shakes of Gavin's head. I wring my hands before realizing that I'm doing pretty much what my mom does when she's stressed.

"A bug told you," the cop says and shares a knowing look

with her partner. "Okay, honey, we'll get you home first and can talk later at the station after you've had a rest and a shower. You have some very worried parents."

The car starts and lights flash. It's pretty cool; I've never been in a cop car with the lights on. Even if the two officers in the front think I'm crazy. The one officer keeps checking on me in the mirror as if she's afraid I'm going to do something strange.

As the car turns down my street, my parents rush out of the house.

"You all right, Gavin?" I ask him as we near.

"Am now," he says. "Sorry I didn't come at first."

We sit and stare at one another for a moment. He lowers his eyes.

"You did come," I say. "Maybe we should go back to Monopoly though?"

Gavin looks back up and grins.

"Sure, just no bugs. That's your thing, not mine."

I smile.

The cops have to open the car door for me, but after that, I'm running and I fling myself into my parents' arms. I'm home, and now that it's over, I am crying.

"I'm sorry," I say. "I'm sorry."

My mother wipes tears from her face, and my father just holds us both. When I clear my eyes, the police are gone with Gavin.

"You should have told us, Jarrod. We would have believed you," my mother says. "We would have."

I can tell that she's trying to convince herself. After my mom finally releases me, my father kneels and grips me by my shoulders.

"We were so worried, Jarrod. You did a very dangerous thing but . . . but I'm proud of you too." He grins, and it's one of his big ones. It lights the night. It's better than any A, any award, any win. "If what I hear is true, you did something really great. You're a hero." He embraces me hard. "But even heroes get in trouble. And you're in trouble."

"But you can keep your bugs," my mom says before I can even ask.

"Really!" I say, pushing out of my father's arms. I don't really care how long they ground me for, as long as I can keep my bugs.

"For now," she says.

"Did you keep Bent? The painted one?" I ask.

"Are you kidding?" my dad says. "We even gave him a little sugar."

"I may have stomped him a little," my mom says. I stare at her, aghast. "What? It was a cockroach. Pink or not, what else was I supposed to do?"

"He's okay," my dad says, and I race inside to check on the real hero of the day.

Epilogue
Where Jarrod Sets His Path

Gavin and I don't play Monopoly the next morning.

We spend most of it back at the police station explaining what happened. I have given up on my bug story, even though I figure I can prove it to them if I really want to. Instead, I just say that I had one my moments near the humming-woman's house, and I guess she'd assumed I had learned about her little business and decided to kidnap me. Gavin confirms that he knew my route home and stopped when he saw my bike. The humming-woman had told him she'd found me unconscious and had me inside on the couch.

Now the woman will get a lot more than a fine for running a puppy mill and cruelty to animals. She's going to jail for two counts of kidnapping and forcible confinement. It's sad to think that she wouldn't even be going to jail if not for kidnapping us.

Everyone wants to know how I trained the roachie to return home for help. That is when a woman tramps into the office and peers at me. With her face inches from mine, her eyes bulge beneath giant glasses. An officer snickers, and I hear someone whisper, *it's the bug-lady.*

"Trained Gromphadorhina portentosa?" she asks. "Hissers?"

I understand what she is asking—whether the roachies are hissing cockroaches.

"Yes, ma'am," I say.

She rubs her wrists together in a way that reminds me of how crickets stridulate, rubbing wings to create their sounds. She does it more like a habit.

"I'd be interested to learn more . . . Bug-boy," she replies. "Bugs are sort of my thing."

She smiles, and I smile back.

"Yes, ma'am."

After she leaves, the officer quips that maybe I should become a junior entomologist. I don't really have much time to think about the comment, not until I am at home and in front of my computer, where I look up the word. That is when I start to get excited.

As I eat dinner that evening, my dad raps me on the helmet. He's all red in the face.

"Jarrod, I—" He grimaces. "It's not really the time, but see, it's time sensitive."

My mom's at the counter cleaning up.

I raise an eyebrow and take another bite of ice cream. He pulls out a little sandwich baggie. As soon as I see it, I push back from the table.

"No way, Dad," I say.

"What?" He dangles the baggie with the speck of a fly inside between his fingertips. "I'm not going to ask this every day, but what you have is amazing."

"No, Dad," I say. "And no, Mom. I'm not eating any more

bugs for you either, not unless it's for something important."

"This is important," my dad says.

"Is it to sell a car?" I ask.

He lowers his hand. "I think one of my colleagues stole a sale."

I hesitate and shake my head. "Life or death. Something major."

His lips purse, and then he claps me on the shoulder. "Good, man," he says. "You're right. You're right." But I can tell he's disappointed I didn't eat the bug.

The next day I sleep in and then watch movies all afternoon. The local newspaper calls and asks for an interview, but I tell them I'm not interested. What I am interested in is school. In fact, I'm thinking about school a little differently now. You see, I learned on the internet that entomologists study bugs. And, the ones who work with police study bugs as they relate to crimes, using their little friends to determine facts about a case. It's like someone has created a job just for me! Unfortunately, my dad was right about one thing: I do need to know about more than just bugs. A lot more. Bug-lady is actually a bug-doctor. I need to become a scientist.

At first, I'm overwhelmed at the thought of becoming good at math and all the different sciences, but when I look at my journal filled with addresses and maps, at my trained bugs, at my sheets of paper where I observed what went on during the moments and recorded them. I realize I can do this. I *can* become a scientist. It's time for me to start believing in myself. And it all starts in eighth grade.

That night, I take some paint thinner and wipe the black

paint from my helmet so that the big bug-eyes are back.

The whole next day, I pay attention in classes, and it doesn't seem as boring as it used to. Okay, some of it is, but not all of it. Mr. Chang doesn't mention our bug discussion. Although I still owe him a detention, news of my kidnapping and my unique method of communicating my location has spread, and the detention isn't even mentioned. Rick calls me Bug-boy every chance he gets, and for the first time I really don't care. Not at all.

"Yes, Rick?" I ask. "You called?" By owning it, I somehow take the power away from him. He stands nonplussed, looking from me to Gavin.

Gavin wants to start a private detection agency, but I'm not sure I'm ready for that yet. And this time it's me who tries hard not to catch Dog-girl's eye. She kept looking over during homeroom, but it's not until afternoon recess that she finally corners me in the yard.

"So now you're a hero," she says, but her eyes are laughing.

"I was pretty scared, actually," I reply.

"I heard you stopped the puppy mill. They're adopting out all the puppies they found in her van and the dogs left in the house. Some of the dogs had never left their cages. Ever."

I don't know what to say. A lot of rumors are flying around. "I'm sorry I got you in trouble."

A little corner of her mouth turns up. It makes me vomit-nervous. "Chang let us out of detention early, but what are you going to do to make it up to me?"

I don't know why I do it. Maybe it's because I know I owe her and I know what she's really asking. "I could take you out, or something?" I ask.

"You're asking me on a date?" She laughs again, and I flush. Maybe I'm wrong. Maybe I should stick with bugs. "All right, but only if you can tell me my name."

I swallow. *Dog-girl.*

"Don't you know your own name?" I stall. I'm sure she's been called upon in class, but it's never registered with me.

She squints and folds her arms across her chest.

There's a certain fly in my wallet that might know. My fingers dip into my shorts, and I feel for the little bump of the bug in the folds of my wallet. Should I do it? I mean, didn't I just tell my parents that I'd only eat bugs if it was *really* important? Life or death. Something major.

"Give me a second," I say and start to kneel. "I feel one of my faints coming on." As I bend down, I bring my palm with the fly to my mouth. But I don't do it.

I sit forward as she leans down toward me, eyes on the tape. "Wait a second, are you trying to learn my name from that bug?" she asks.

"Gavin told you."

She nods. "He doesn't hold up well under torture."

I shake my head.

She helps me to my feet. "This bug eating is for real? You can see their memories?"

I nod, but put a finger to my lips.

"That's so cool," she whispers. "And you really don't know my name?"

"Dog-girl?" I cringe.

She glances at her dress and picks some fur from it. "Good enough for me, but you know what?" I shake my head. "My friends call me Ketura. Ketty for short."

I resist the urge to play dead like a clown beetle. "It's nice to meet you, Ketty. . . . Do you want to meet my bugs?"

The tumult of the yard full of kids fades into the background as I wait for an answer. Blood throbs in my ears.

"Only if I can introduce you to Ralph."

"Ralph?" I ask.

"He's a retired cadaver dog I'm adopting."

"Cadaver—as in human corpse?" I draw back a step.

"He finds people," she says.

"Yeah, dead people."

"Sometimes. But usually it's just porkchops."

I laugh. "Doesn't sound like a very good cadaver dog."

"Ralph might have been retired for a reason." Ketty sighs.

"I'd love to meet Ralph," I say. The school bell rings, and kids flow about us as if we're a rock in a rushing river.

Ketty grabs the sleeve of my shirt and pulls me into the throng. "Between your bugs and my dog, maybe we should start a detective agency?"

It's funny, but for some reason, coming from Ketty, a detective agency's beginning to sound like a *really* good idea.

Acknowledgements

This book would not have been possible without the efforts and support of a great number of people. To my editing team of Catherine Adams, Jessica Holland, Stephanie Parent and Gina Panettieri, thank you for exercising the diligence I lack. To Jason Anderson for formatting, to Martin Stiff at Amazing15 for the awesome cover, and to Glendon Haddix for the print version—presentation is everything and books are judged by their covers every day. To the Odyssey Writers Workshop, the Sunnyside Writers Group, and all my Facebook friends who weigh in on important decisions, where would I be without others to share the pain and joy of this writing world?

Finally, to my girls and my wife (thank you for never chewing off my head!), you are my first readers. My maggots. My thing. And I love you.

Thank you, dear Reader. Now, if I could 'bug' you for one more thing.

If you enjoyed this book and would like to review it, please do, wherever you make purchases. There are no greater gifts to an author than reviews and word of mouth.

You can find me on Amazon, Goodreads, Facebook, and Twitter. I love to talk.

If you'd like to hear about new releases and take part in giveaways or opportunities to act as an advance reader, please sign up to my newsletter on my website or via my Facebook page. You'll get a free book. ☺

About the Author

Michael is an award winning author who lives in Ottawa, Canada. His graphic novels, novels, and early readers have been published by Rubicon Publishing and distributed by Pearson Education, Scholastic, and Oxford University Press. To learn more about Michael and his projects, visit his website at www.michaelfstewart.com.

CPSIA information can be obtained
at www.ICGtesting.com
Printed in the USA
LVHW04s1620200418
574264LV00002B/369/P